D0290301

*This book is dedicated to all pets
and their devoted owners.*

CONTENTS

INTRODUCTION

Ever since I can remember, all that I have ever wanted to do is save the animals. I have the great luck and fortune to be living out my lifelong dream of practicing veterinary medicine and surgery. Because of this passion, I tend to spend a lot of time with my clients, explaining as much as possible, and recommending a lot of preventative care. Because I can only reach a limited number of pet owners by practicing in animal hospitals and clinics, I wanted to help more pet owners. WCBS 880 news radio, in New York City, afforded me that opportunity. I have been writing and recording "Healthy & Happy Pet" reports since 2004. How challenging to limit my scripts to 60 seconds, especially since I have so much to say! It's a good thing that I speak very fast. This is the New Yorker in me.

This book is a compilation of more than twenty years of experiences that have happened in the veterinary clinics and hospitals where I have worked. Each day has been a learning experience. Knowledge empowers pet owners. Providing that knowledge helps me to keep pet owners informed and their animal companions, both those who do and do not wear fur, healthy and happy.

CHAPTER ONE

Have I Got A Job For You!

One of my clients pleasantly greets me as I enter through the front door. With her dog sitting peacefully in her lap she says to me, "Good morning, Dr. Cohen." I return the greeting. The waiting room is filling up with patients. As I pass the receptionist, I overhear her answering the telephone. Alice says, "Doctor's office, may I help you? Excuse me; you want the telephone number of the pizza place across the street from us? Do you need an appointment for your pet? You can call information ma'am. O.K., O.K., 718-555-1713. No, I don't know what the specials are ma'am!"

I have been practicing veterinary medicine and surgery since 1988. I love being a veterinarian and there is not a day that goes by that I am not truly grateful for what I do. I always knew how mentally stimulating and challenging it would be, but I had no idea how entertaining this field is!

After checking on hospital patients and doing morning treatments, I am ready to see my first client. She waits for me in exam room number one. Her dog has been weighed and her temperature taken, the dog's that is. As I enter the room, I notice that Mrs. Klinger has a frightened look on her face. Client card in hand, I ask her, "What seems to be the problem with Fluffy?" Mrs. Klinger answers, "Oh, my Fluffy has no problem; she is just here for her booster shots. It is that loud client in the waiting room.

She frightened my poor puppy with her ranting."

Out of sheer curiosity, I peek out the side window to see what Mrs. Klinger is talking about. I see a very determined middle-aged woman wearing a dress that is buttoned to the very top of her neck. She holds an English-German dictionary in one hand and points her finger up and down at her dog with the other hand. This client is actually barking out orders to her dog in German! Her dog happens to be a German Shepherd. I excuse myself from the exam room to calm down this client who is now screaming at her dog in the waiting room. Not only is she upsetting the other clients and pets, she is making her own dog extremely nervous. I gently suggest to her that she can train her dog using English commands. You would think that this is an obvious deduction. How could someone actually believe that you must learn a new language to better communicate with your pet? Common sense is obviously out the window. However, this has happened to me before. Several years ago I had a client who asked me if he had to learn Japanese because his new puppy was an Akita, a Japanese dog. Pets can sometimes make the most otherwise seemingly intelligent people say and do the strangest things!

So now I know two people who think that they have to adopt the native language of their dogs' breeds. I guess this is not as far-fetched as two other clients I know who talk to their dogs and actually believe that their dogs talk back to them and in English, no less!

One, Mrs. Palchek, has four children. She was telling me about a fight that two of her children were having. One called the other one a moron or something and, of course, that one retaliated with another slur. It took me about five minutes into the conversation to realize that she was talking about her dogs! I did not realize that she also considered her dogs, her children. Mrs. Palchek is an Ivy League educated woman, very well-versed in English literature. She once told her human son that the dogs called her by name. She tells me that her son did not believe her until he witnessed this for himself. At first, I thought that she was pulling my leg but she was QUITE serious. She really did believe that these dogs called her by name and, of course, spoke to each other in English.

Another client, Mrs. Smith, not only talks to her dogs, but also moves their lips and speaks out of the corner of her mouth as if to answer for them. I try to maintain my composure when I see her.

Let us get back to poor Mrs. Klinger and her Fluffy still waiting for me in exam room number one. I enter the room; both client and patient finally calm, and I proceed with the examination. I always like a calm client. If the client is upset, the patient will sense this and may become upset him or herself. The exam is probably the most important first step in making a correct diagnosis. Even for routine boosters, a thorough exam is a must. I ask the standard questions – is there any coughing or sneezing? Does your pet have any vomiting or diarrhea? Is he or she drinking and eating normally? Can he or she jump on and off the couch? If all is fine, I start the exam at the tip of the nose and work my way back to the tail end. I look into the eyes and ears, mouth and throat. I percuss the sinuses. That is, I tap on the head to hear a clear sound resonating back. I volunteer an explanation to the owners beforehand. I tell them that I am not just hitting their beloved pet in the head, but I am actually evaluating whether the sinuses are clear or not. Many head colds have been discovered this way. I also percuss the chest. Some cases of pneumonia or fluid in the chest would sound quiet or clear on auscultation but dull on percussion. In other words, when I move my stethoscope over the area that has the pneumonia or fluid, I hear nothing. But when I percuss that same area, tap my fingers over the chest wall, I hear dullness. This dullness is what alerts me to the possibility of pneumonia, collapsed lung, tumor or fluid-filled lungs.

Besides looking down the throat, I palpate or feel the outside of the neck. I feel and note the size and shape of the lymph nodes and check the thyroid glands. I next move onto the abdomen. I love feeling the belly of a thin animal. One advantage to palpating a thin animal is the ability to feel the size and shape of individual organs. When you can feel so much detail, it makes it easy to find a problem. With fat animals, there can be layers of fat that hide the individual organs underneath, and the fat can actually mask a problem. The fat may make you miss a diagnosis because it literally gets in the way. I recommend taking radiographs or x-rays of all animals that are obese and have vomiting and/or diarrhea signs. The fat may make it difficult to evaluate the stomach and intestines during an examination, but it does provide a wonderful contrast on x-rays. Fat animals have better-defined x-rays than thin ones. And besides, any dog or cat that has a stomach ache will not let you feel his or her belly properly simply because it hurts. X-rays should always be taken on pets that make a muscle and guard their abdomens so that you can better evaluate what is going on inside.

Getting back to the examination, I do simple neurological evaluations like turning a head up and down and side to side to evaluate the positioning of the eyes. I turn over a paw to make sure the dog or cat can flip it back again properly. I like to watch an animal walk into the room, especially one that presents with a limp. A trip to the veterinarian's office can create anxiety and fear in some pets. While in the hospital environment, a pet can have so much adrenaline flowing that he or she will not feel any minor aches or pains that were felt at home while in a more relaxing and comforting environment. In fact, unless your dog or cat has a serious limp, one caused by a very painful problem like a broken bone, severe hip dysplasia or a ruptured knee ligament, your pet could end up running into the examination room because the adrenaline surge could temporarily numb the pain. If a client feels that the limp was a psychological trick to get attention or a treat, then that very same pet that ran into the exam room will go home and limp all over again, if nothing is done to diagnose and treat the problem. I cannot tell you how many times I have clients tell me that they brought their pet into the hospital because of a limp at home. As soon as they arrive, the owners become upset to see that same pet that was limping at home, running around the hospital waiting room. Some clients actually believe that their pet was faking the limp for attention. Some animals do this in the wild. Birds can feign a broken wing to distract a predator away from the nest. When the predator is far enough away, the bird then flies away. I can assure you that pets do not fake limps. If your pet is limping, a medical reason lies behind it. Sometimes, it is as simple as a foreign body like a piece of glass or a splinter in the footpad. All limping pets should be taken seriously and properly examined.

Continuing with the examination, I note if a male or female has been neutered. Unless an animal is going to be bred, I always recommend neutering. For females, an ovariohysterectomy, or spay, decreases the chance of breast cancer and completely eliminates the chances of ovarian, uterine and cervical cancer, and prevents the formation of a pyometra, a life-threatening infection of the uterus. In males, an orchiectomy, or castration, decreases the chances of prostate cancer and infections, perianal tumors (growths around the anus) and completely eliminates the chances of testicular cancer and torsion (a very painful twisting of the testicle). When I have a macho client in the room who looks insulted if I recommend castration, I try to be as gentle as possible. Sometimes, I will refer him to one of the male veterinarians and make sure that I tell him that it is nothing personal; I encourage female pets to be spayed, as well.

I once had a client drop off her dog for a neuter and she actually asked me if the "pink thing" was still going to be there! I explained to her that I was just going to remove the testicles and not the penis! The scrotum was going to stay there as well, just a little emptier. I always make a note in the patient's record that I recommended neutering. Sometimes, the same clients who get upset or insulted by the recommendation of a neutering surgery can be the same ones that come back to you if the female gets a uterine infection or the male ends up with prostate cancer and say that no one ever recommended the preventative surgery. When this happens, I never say, "I told you so." Everyone feels bad enough as it is.

One client of mine had a male German Shorthaired Pointer that I recommended neutering eight years ago. His dog developed a severe prostate infection. We did an ultrasound exam of the abdomen, and though the prostate was very enlarged, it looked free of cancer. I recommended two weeks of antibiotics and on the second week, scheduling the neutering. He was very upset with me for even mentioning the surgery and said, "Dr. Cohen, you are trying to take away his masculinity. His personality is going to change. He loves to lick his balls; what will he do now?" I wasn't worried about the infection, because I knew that the antibiotics would cure it. My concern was the size of the prostate; it was huge! There are only two ways to shrink an enlarged prostate. The first way is to use female hormone injections or pills, but this choice of treatment poses a serious risk. Giving female hormones like estrogen to any patient can cause the bone marrow to stop producing red blood cells. If it suppresses the bone marrow severely enough, then white blood cells and platelets could also stop being produced. This is called anemia if it just affects the red blood cells and bone marrow aplasia, if it affects all of the blood cells. The second way is much safer. Castration, permanently removing both testicles, will shrink an enlarged prostate within two weeks from the surgery.

Mr. Sicilia loved his dog, but this was not just any dog. He was a hunting dog. Thank God he was more worried about his dog's health than his hunting buddies' comments. He told me, "Doc, I will do the surgery, but I don't want Rocky to look like he had his you-know-whats taken out. Can you fix him like that?"

I don't care one way or the other when it comes to testicular implants. They are sterilized hard plastic or solid silicone kidney-shaped inserts. They don't change shape and are used for the owner's benefit only. If someone were to enter a neutered male dog with testicular implants into a dog show competition, he would be disqualified. One of the competition criteria that the dog must meet is that he must still be intact, and the judge will feel for the testicles. It is the client's choice whether to put in implants or not. Putting in testicular implants does add to the cost of the surgery. If the client wants the dog to look more natural, besides testicular implants, the surgery can be performed so that the scrotum is not left completely empty. When doing a castration, the surgeon wants to tie and cut off, or ligate, the vessels leading to the testicle as far away from the testicle as possible. This leads to little or no bleeding from the stump left behind. However, if you want the scrotum to look as if something is still there, you can tie off the vessels closer to the testicle. After you tie off the vessels and cut the testicle off, you leave behind a stump, but because it is closer to the end, a hematoma or blood clot can form. I do not perform a neuter surgery this way unless the owner is very determined to have a male dog look as if he still has his testicles. Most of the time, a surgeon does not want to create a hematoma, but it does look more natural once everything else has healed. In reality, no male dog, neutered or intact, will allow you to walk up to him and feel his scrotum to see if it is full or empty. Therefore, most people are satisfied with the normal outcome. Mr. Sicilia allowed me to neuter his dog, but swore me to secrecy. His name was changed to protect his secret from his hunting buddies. Rocky has never had another prostate infection; his prostate gland shrunk tremendously; and he is happily hunting and licking his fake you-know-whats. And his personality remained the same!

Getting back to the examination, I take a look at the skin, after addressing the gender of the animal. I don't worry about removing wart-like growths on old dogs and cats unless one of the three following criteria are met: first, they have changed in size, shape or color since the last exam; second, they bother the owner and/or pet; or third, they are rubbing on the eye. With any of the aforementioned, wart-like growths should be surgically removed. As animals get older, they get the occasional lump or bump and I point these growths out to the owner and make a notation in the record. If at anytime, one of these growths do change, then it should be removed and biopsied to make sure it is not malignant.

Last but not least, I examine the tail and rear end. Pelvic examinations are often overlooked. I always tell the owners that people are not the only ones that do not like to get a digital examination. I don't enjoy doing this exam, nor do I think that the patient enjoys having it done. Yet, this is a very important examination to do.

First of all, this is the only way to evaluate the anal sacs or glands. These are vestigial organs in all dogs and cats. Some animals can express them at will, but many cannot. These muscles have weakened over time from lack of use. The wild ancestors of domesticated pets used these glands to mark their territory and attract mates. Skunks still have control over their anal glands and can express them at will to ward off predators. In fact, this is why the anal glands in pets are sometimes called the "skunk glands." They produce the most foul, offensive, rotten-smelling secretions. However, without a digital examination, these glands cannot be properly evaluated. If you ever see your pet rubbing his or her butt across the floor, that is a red flag for you to make an appointment for your pet to see the veterinarian and have the anal glands checked. By having your pet's anal glands expressed, you can prevent a painful abscess from forming and you will be giving him or her relief. Anal sacs can fill up and cause discomfort and itching. Some dogs need to have their anal glands expressed on a regular basis. Some dogs have such anal gland problems that they need to have them surgically removed.

Secondly, growths inside the anus can be found. Many times, rectal and anal gland tumors are missed because they are not looked for. By gloving up, and inserting a lubricated finger into an animal's rectum, I have found many tumors before they had a chance to become problems.

Lastly, I can get a fecal sample if the owner forgot to bring one. I warn owners that their pet may squirm or even cry during this part of the exam, but it is a necessary procedure. On that note, I finish the exam. By making sure your pet has been thoroughly examined, you can have peace of mind in knowing that you have a healthy pet.

Every once in a while, I will enter an exam room and ask the client if he or she brought in a stool sample. If I get one handed to me, I usually joke. "Oh, you brought me a gift. We love these kinds of presents." I then hand off the specimen to the veterinary technician.

Occasionally, I have foreign clients and it is obvious that English is not their first language. They can get by with most of the exam questions, but this confused look comes across their faces when I ask them if they brought in a stool sample. I go through the entire list of synonyms for feces until something rings a bell. I start off asking, "Do you have a stool sample? Fecal sample? Poop? Doo doo? Poo poo? Caca?..." Eventually, the confused looks change to smiles. Apparently, everyone finds bathroom humor funny. I try and stay as professional as possible, but if you enter the exam room when I am down to "caca," you cannot help but laugh. I had one client look at me and say very seriously in a heavy accent, "Oh, you mean the shit!"

Once, I had a client who named his cat "Shithead." I tried to say things like, "How has 'your cat' been feeling?" Or "Has 'your cat' had any vomiting or diarrhea?" The client was almost insulted that I would not call his cat by his given name. In fact, I sometimes call in my patients from the waiting room myself. "Fluffy Klinger, you are next. Please come into exam room number one," I might say. Shithead Gonzalez was the exception. I just could not bring myself to having a professional and serious conversation with Mr. Gonzalez by saying, "So, how has Shithead been feeling?" I try to stay as objective as possible, especially when it comes to personal decisions like a pet's name, but I could not contain myself any longer. I asked, "Mr. Gonzalez, why would you call your cat... why would you name your cat... what possessed you to choose your cat's name?" He answered me, "It's quite simple. When I got him as a kitten, I went through the naming book. I called him one name after another and got nothing, no response. After trying this for hours and literally going through every single name in the book, I finally gave up and said, 'Hey, Shithead, get over here!' and he came running. It was the only name that he would respond to. So, if anything, it was he who chose his name, not I!" How can you argue with that logic?

CHAPTER TWO

Strange Events

While my first client of the day is filling out a new patient information card at the front desk, I overhear her asking Alice, the receptionist, if the hospital needs her social security number or the cat's. Alice tells the client that we need the human social security number and answers the phone, "Doctor's office, may I help you?" She hands me the phone and says, "The caller has a doctor's question." I say, "Dr. Cohen speaking, how may I help you?" The caller asks, "How do you spell hip dysplasia?" My reply, "I would be happy to spell it for you, but it is in the dictionary." In a very arrogant tone of voice the caller says to me, "Doc, if I knew how to spell the word, I could have looked it up myself instead of calling you!"

I respond, "H-I-P, new word, D-Y-S-P-L-A-S-I-A." As I am hanging up the receiver, the client filling out the paperwork turns to me and asks, "Since you are such a good speller, how do you spell A.S.P.C.A.?" I reply, "A-S-P-C-A." "Oh, thank you!" she says, in a serious tone, no less. "I adopted this cat yesterday and she is very old, can she have a senior citizen's discount?" Now I feel as if I have just entered the Twilight Zone. I reply, "If your cat pays the bill herself, then she is entitled to a senior citizen's discount; if you are paying the bill, then you will have to wait about another twenty years!"

I have a technician weigh and take the temperature of Ms. Reynolds' cat while I go through my usual questioning about eating, drinking, and movement habits. Geriatric cats, and dogs for that matter, have special needs just like older people. It is important to note if the appetite has lessened or increased, or the pet is drinking and urinating more frequently, this could alert you to early signs of disease. Older cats and dogs may not be able to jump on and off the couch like they used to; they may not hear or see as well; they may sleep more. All of the above are normal aging changes. Provided that the appetite is still good and drinking and urinating is the same, it is still a good idea to get baseline blood work, urinalysis and x-rays. This way, if something does change, you can compare the new results with the previous baseline tests and perhaps detect a problem early. Timely diagnosis of any disease leads to earlier treatment and better chances of a cure.

Ms. Reynolds did not have her cat long enough to establish daily routines yet, but she did think that her new, old cat acted young for her age. This new cat did not have a name yet, but Ms. Reynolds thought that she acted very nervous. A new environment for an old cat could cause this reaction, the personality of the cat may be one of nervousness, or a disease could be present.

Interestingly enough, when I hold the ophthalmoscope up to one of the eyes for an ocular examination, I notice a blood clot in the retina, the back of the eye. This kind of examination is called a fundic exam.

The back of dog and cat eyes look like works of art. There is a central white circle, which is where the optic nerve attaches; then, there are networks of red lines branching out, which are the retinal vessels. They branch across a fluorescent green background, which is spectacular in color. Instead of smooth, thin red lines branching out, the retinal vessels in Ms. Reynolds' cat had red blotches indicative of blood clots. The number one reason for blood clots in the back of the eye is high blood pressure or hypertension. This could be a solitary disease process or could be connected with another disease like hyperthyroidism or kidney disease. I measure systemic blood pressure the same way a medical doctor would measure a person's pressure. There are different size cuffs and I place the appropriate size cuff around one of the limbs. When Ms. Reynolds' cat's blood pressure was taken, it was indeed high. There are medications to lower the blood pressure, but I also wanted to assess the rest of the blood tests to rule out other diseases. Ms. Reynolds' cat was hyperthyroid and had the very earliest changes consistent with kidney disease.

Here is an example of the patient not reading the book. Typical hyperthyroid cats can have vomiting and/or diarrhea, and eat voraciously and yet lose weight. This cat was not particularly thin, did not have an enormous appetite, and there was no vomiting or diarrhea.

Kidney-diseased animals usually will drink and urinate more, tend to eat less, and seek warm places. The kidneys normally regulate the amount of water and electrolytes in the body. An animal in kidney failure loses this ability. The failure of the kidneys to filter the blood properly causes the animal to urinate in greater volume with decreased concentration. These patients are in a constant state of dehydration. The waste products that normally get filtered out into the urine stay in the blood and can make the patient nauseous. This accounts for the decreased appetite. The kidneys make a hormone called erythropoietin, which is responsible for making red blood cells. Kidney failure patients can be anemic due to the lack of this hormone. Dehydration and anemia can lead to colder extremities and so these animals tend to seek heat. You may see a dog or cat with kidney disease staying next to the radiator or stove. That is, if they read the book. Other diseases, such as heart disease, can also leave a pet with colder extremities. The failure of proper circulation or low blood pressure can lead to the same results. Always keep in mind, any sudden change in pet behavior, like seeking out warmth, could indicate a medical problem.

Ms. Reynolds' cat did very well on her blood pressure and hyperthyroid medications. On repeat blood and urine tests, everything was in the normal range, even the kidneys! Lucky enough, Ms. Reynolds' cat did just fine.

Later Ms. Reynolds had returned for a six-month follow-up examination at which time I also wanted to take blood from Shasta. (She named the cat shortly after her first visit.) As I was preparing to take blood from the cat, I noticed that Ms. Reynolds started rolling up one of her sleeves. "Excuse me, what are you doing?" I asked her. "Well, you are always so gentle with Shasta and my internist told me that I needed to get a blood test so..." "I don't do humans," I interrupted. "I am sure you can find a gentle phlebotomist at your doctor's office."

Taking blood from animals can be challenging. I have to make sure that the patient is comfortable while being restrained. In order to see the vein, I soak the leg or neck with alcohol to wet the hair down sufficiently. In very fat animals, I go almost exclusively by feel, I palpate where the vein is. If I need a lot of blood (5 cc, the equivalent of 1 teaspoon) I like to use the jugular vein. At first, many clients gasp at this suggestion looking at me as if I were a vampire, but interestingly enough this is probably the gentlest and quickest way to take blood. First of all, there are less nerve endings in the neck than the front leg, so the patient won't feel it as much. Secondly, the jugular vein (neck vein) is much larger than the cephalic vein (front leg vein) so that the blood flows into the syringe faster and is less likely to clot. And finally, the patient does not see the needle entering his or her leg, which could create anxiety in itself. On the whole, the patient is much more comfortable provided that the client does not stress out. I always explain why I like to take the blood out of the neck prior to performing the act. If someone is so horrified by this method, I use the leg.

One day, I had a six-foot five-inch, three hundred and fifty pound client with tattoos on his arm come in with his dog for a blood test. I always ask ahead of time if the client has any problem with watching me take blood or if he or she would be more comfortable stepping out of the room. I asked Mr. Chase this and he was insulted. "In Vietnam, I carried bodies back with missing parts without batting an eye and you are asking me if seeing my dog's blood is going to bother me!" I quickly apologized and explained that I once had an elderly gentleman pass out and hit the floor while I was taking blood from his cat, so I ask everyone ahead of time. I told him not to take it personally.

I had the technician hold the dog's front leg out while rolling the vein. For a small amount of blood, I normally use the technician's thumb as a tourniquet since the procedure is a very quick one. I applied some alcohol; inserted the needle and pulled back on the plunger of the syringe watching it fill up with deep, rich, red blood. All of a sudden, I heard a loud thud against the wall and then on the floor. I looked up and saw that this big, brawny client hit his head on the wall and fell onto the floor. I broke out into a nervous sweat. The last client that passed out got up almost immediately. Thirty seconds have passed and I was ready to call 911. No sooner did I pick up the phone, did I hear Mr. Chase asking, "How did I get on the floor, why does my head hurt and why are my jeans wet?" I advised Mr. Chase to seek medical attention. He was so embarrassed I never saw him again. Animals are easy, but people .... I am glad that I am a veterinarian!

CHAPTER THREE

Stranger Events

People say that truth is stranger than fiction and I have to agree. Some client comments like "I think that my cat is smarter than the President," may not be all that far-fetched depending on who is in the White House at the time, but "Doctor, you know that dog spelled backwards is God, and that's who she is!" definitely falls under the above category.

Over the years, I have had some awkward moments in which clients give me more information than I need to know about themselves and not their pets. I have one client waiting for me in exam room number one. The receptionist informs me that she has no pet with her; she just wants to ask me a question. As I enter the exam room, she removes her shirt. She points to some lesion on her chest and says to me, "Pretend that I am a dog or a cat, tell me what this is and how I should treat it!" I politely asked her to put her shirt back on and see her dermatologist. I explained to her that I am licensed to practice VETERINARY medicine, not HUMAN medicine.

Coincidently, the client in exam room number two, greets me in the hallway, just outside of the exam room. She tells me that her eighteen-year old son has crabs. As I enter the room, thank goodness, I only see her dog. She asks me to examine the dog, convinced that he is the cause of her son's louse problem. I examine the dog from head to toe and do a louse check for completeness. However, I explain that lice are species-specific. Dog lice only go to other dogs and people lice only go to other people. They do not cross species lines. I am not going to get any more specific than that. There is no need to go into details about the differences between crabs, which are sexually transmitted lice, versus head lice that get transmitted by kids who share hats, combs and headphones.

Just when you think things can't get any more embarrassing, I have an experience with my next client and her sick iguana. Most exotic animal problems stem from poor husbandry like improper feeding or a poor environment. The questions I ask exotic pet owners have more to do with the type of housing, bedding, heat source, food and water supply they are offering their pet. For example, I see a lot of burns on snakes and lizards from hot rocks. In the wild, reptiles and amphibians get warm by lying out in the sun. Sometimes, they lie on a rock and bask. They need to bask to regulate their body temperature for proper digestion and a good-working immune system. A heat source in a cage or aquarium should come from an incandescent light source and an ultraviolet light kept in the corner so that a temperature gradient is created, warmest by the corner where the light is (95 degrees Fahrenheit) and coolest at the other end (85 degrees Fahrenheit). The problem with hot rocks in aquariums is that their heat is not evenly distributed. The electric coil inside the rock creates a hot spot that can burn the skin and underlying tissue. A rock in the wild, heated up naturally from the sun, is never too hot to cause a burn and the heat is evenly distributed. Besides, reptiles get their heat from the sun and not the rock. Reptiles warm up by maintaining a body temperature that is 10 degrees higher than the ambient temperature. Providing a temperature gradient that is warmest at one end allows the reptile to lie in the appropriate spot. This can never happen with a hot rock or a heating pad. The reptile will lie on it to the point of a burn and may never even achieve his or her preferred optimal temperature zone.

The safest, cheapest and cleanest bedding is newspaper. It can be changed daily and there is no need to worry about mites or other contaminants that some bedding sources might contain. There should be proper ventilation. Two parallel sides of the glass of an aquarium can be knocked out and replaced with pegboard so that cross ventilation can occur. Screened housing is great for proper ventilation, but very difficult to maintain high temperatures. Therefore, if screened cages are used for reptiles, the ambient room temperature needs to be kept much higher. Screened housing is not a good housing for snakes or iguanas because they tend to rub their faces raw on the screen. There should be some sort of hiding place and climbing area and a large bowl of water, large enough for soaking and changed on a daily basis. Having a large bowl of water also provides the environment with proper humidity. Feedings, types of food and frequency, varies depending on the species.

Another common problem I see with snakes and other carnivorous reptiles is bite wounds. I tell my clients that it is always safest to teach a captive snake to eat a thawed out frozen mouse instead of a live one. With live prey, if the snake is not hungry, the prey could take a bite or two out of the predator. These snakes come in with painful, infected bite wounds that many times are lethal, and could have been prevented in the first place. It is easy to train them. A person can take a pair of very long tongs and hold the thawed out frozen mouse in them. He or she then teases the snake by dangling the mouse in front of the snake up and down and back and forth until eliciting a feeding response. Most hungry snakes will lunge at a moving prey item. Obviously, one should never hold the mouse with his or her fingers because if the snake lunges, he or she could be bitten. All snakes have very sharp teeth and produce painful bites. Small or young snakes eat baby mice called pinkies. Larger snakes eat adult rodents. Adult mice have full bone development, offering a good calcium source. A person can insert vitamins into the killed prey item if better nutrition is needed during a growth spurt. He or she should not overuse vitamins and minerals with exotics. Sometimes, too much can be just as harmful or even worse than too little.

Ms. Crum kept Iggy, the iguana, in a very small aquarium with a hot rock and a regular light bulb. After my husbandry discussion, I look at Iggy. On physical examination, Iggy is extremely thin and badly dehydrated. There is water kept in the cage, but not large enough for Iggy to soak in. Dehydrated iguanas cannot absorb water directly through their skin because of their scales; but if they soak, they can absorb some water through the cloaca and of course, by drinking. Iggy needs additional fluids.

Correcting the husbandry problem is only part of the solution. Iggy is also being fed lettuce, not a very nutritious food. I don't know an iguana that doesn't like dandelions, strawberries or bok choy. They should be offered a variety of fruits and vegetables; they are herbivores. Never give spinach because it binds to calcium leading to metabolic bone disease. Be careful not to offer too much cabbage, cauliflower and broccoli because these vegetables can decrease thyroid function. Lettuce has the least nutritional value and iceberg lettuce is the worst. Dark, leafy green vegetables are the best, high in calcium and low in phosphrus.

Because Iggy is so badly dehydrated, I need to give him subcutaneous fluids. I explain to Ms. Crum that I am going to insert the needle under Iggy's skin and that a bubble will appear where the fluids enter. This bubble will go down as Iggy absorbs the fluids. It is not going to be painful or uncomfortable for the iguana. After explaining all of the above, I proceed with the treatment. Ms. Crum looks a little pale and I am concerned about her passing out. I recommend that she sit down or turn her head in another direction, if watching me treat Iggy was going to upset her in anyway. She opens her mouth as if she is about to say something and all of a sudden proceeds to vomit violently all over the technician, the examination table, her beloved Iggy, the iguana and me. After this, she is the only one in that room that felt better. Needless to say, I have had better days.

Everyone knows that reptiles have a defense mechanism where their tails can detach or break off when a predator catches them by the tail. In some species of reptiles, they can even grow back a new tail. The tails of iguanas that break off do not grow back as they do with geckos. Interestingly enough, leopard geckos can consciously drop their tails in order to escape a predator, even if the predator doesn't touch their tails! There is a very special and unique distraction method when a reptile's tail does detach. It starts to whip around and distract the predator, while the now tailless reptile can escape. I know this, but still am not prepared for the surprise I have during a surgery on an anesthetized iguana with a very badly infected tail.

Wanda is a very large iguana; she is seven years old and her tail is infected at the base. Wanda's owner tried topical antibiotics, even antibiotic injections every three days, but the infection became worse. The circulation became poorer and the pain became greater. The owner finally agrees to an amputation surgery. I am not prepared for what happens next. Wanda is intubated, an endotracheal tube is passed down her trachea and she is maintained on isofluorane gas anesthesia and oxygen. After the surgery site is prepared, I proceed to cut off the tail where there is still healthy tissue. I do a wedge resection so that the two ends left can be sewn back together and the tail will end up healing and looking almost like a fish, scales and all. As I make the final cut, the tail starts to whip and thrash around like a snake out of control. It startles me! I know about this defense mechanism and how the detached tail can distract a predator in the wild, but I do not expect this from an anesthetized reptilian patient. During surgery, I am very serious and entirely focused on the patient. When this tail starts whipping out of control, I am just grateful that I do not suffer from a heart attack!

I think the day would end on a high note when I overhear the receptionist speaking to someone on the phone regarding a twenty-five foot snake. I say to myself, "I have never treated such a big snake before. This, undoubtedly must be some kind of anaconda or python; I don't think boas get that large." I become very excited at such a challenge. I start to prepare for this adventure by checking my snake books regarding anacondas and pythons, specifically. As soon as Alice hangs up the phone, I question her about when this exciting patient is coming in. She gives me a very perplexed gaze. "What patient are you referring to, Dr. Cohen?" "The twenty-five foot snake, of course," I reply. She starts to laugh. "This has been a very long day. I just got off the phone with the plumber who suggested that we use a twenty-five foot snake to unclog the drain," Alice explains.

Just when you think things can't get any stranger I hear John, the technician, screaming. Leanne, a cat that has just been rescued herself, decides to take a bite out of John's butt. This is a seemingly sweet cat. That is, if a cat is not being held down. Apparently, if one of her fellow cats is vocalizing in any way while restrained, Leanne will come to his or her aid, and attack the person holding down the sick cat. Whether a vet is taking blood, giving medications, applying a cast or even trimming nails, if Leanne thinks that he or she is hurting a member of her species, she will courageously take it upon herself to attack. For some reason, she is partial to butts. Since Leanne has free range of the hospital, she has to get kenneled when a cat needs any kind of diagnostic work-up or treatment. If I am working on a dog, Leanne is not fazed. I guess truth is stranger than fiction!

CHAPTER FOUR

Puppy Love And Kitty Care

It seems to be pediatrics week at the hospital, lately. I usually see a new puppy or kitten on a regular basis, but for whatever reason, there seems to be a glut of juveniles today. I have a new puppy in exam room number one and a new kitten in exam room number two. I especially like to examine new puppies and kittens because they don't possess any doctor fears yet. As I enter exam room number one, I greet the puppy in a high-pitched voice, "Well, hello there little girl!" The puppy rolls onto her back, the tail begins to wag furiously, while she proceeds to urinate on the examination table. Only a true animal lover can appreciate this joyful meeting without becoming ill. Mrs. Cantor is beaming. She could not be any prouder; it is almost as if she had given birth to Jillian herself. Jillian is an extremely healthy, six-week old Golden Retriever. I examine her from head to toe and find nothing wrong with her. With every new puppy and kitten I examine, I go through an informative monologue with the owner.

Getting a new puppy or kitten in many ways resembles having a new baby, human that is. They tend to sleep lot, you have to safety proof your home, and you need to teach them what is acceptable behavior and what is not.

I encourage the entire family to work with the new puppy or kitten. "Open the mouth often, especially during a meal, and actually remove some food from the mouth with your fingers," I say. I get the same reaction from every person I tell this to, sheer puzzlement, but it is an important exercise that should be done daily with every new puppy or kitten for a very good reason. I continue, "When your dog or cat is full-grown, and a chicken or fish bone falls off the table and onto the floor, your adult pet will pounce on it. Or, if your dog tries to eat something dangerous found on the street during a walk, it is important to be able to safely remove that object without getting growled at or bitten. If swallowed, an object can cause severe problems, anything from vomiting and/or bloody diarrhea to a blockage in the digestive tract. Sharpened edges from a chewed bone can cut on the way down and even cause a puncture. Something picked up from the street and swallowed could cause illness or poisoning. It is so much safer for your pet and easier for you to be able to put your hands into the mouth and retrieve the object before it can cause a problem. If you practice opening up your pet's mouth when he or she is young, your pet will become used to it and will not bite you if you try this act on him or her as an adult."

An example of what can happen when you do not train your pet properly and cannot take food away from his or her mouth, happened several years ago. On an emergency basis, I saw a grown dog brought in with severe burns down the throat and in the stomach. Interestingly enough, the mouth was fine. He had swallowed a hot potato and the dog never allowed the owners to get near him when he had food. This would never have been the case, if he were used to having the owners open up his mouth and remove food early on.

I also encourage brushing the puppy's or kitten's teeth. As juveniles they are teething. Their gums are sore, losing baby teeth and getting adult teeth. Brushing the teeth when a pet is young serves two purposes: first, it massages the gums; second, your pet becomes accustomed to the whole brushing process. It is much easier to introduce a toothbrush or finger brush to a puppy or kitten than a full-grown dog or cat.

The toothpastes come in different flavors like chicken or seafood and are digestible so you don't even need to rinse! In fact, the paste works best by not rinsing because it contains enzymes which dissolve dental tartar and remove plaque. The longer the toothpaste is left on the teeth and gums, the better it works. Some are even fortified with fluoride! If puppies and kittens get used to having their teeth brushed when they are young, they not only tolerate it as an adult, they expect it. You don't have to brush three times daily; once a day will suffice.

A common misconception is that feeding dry food will clean your pet's teeth. In reality, there is no difference between feeding canned or dry food when it comes to having cleaner teeth unless the dry food is a tartar-control formula. This type of food is actually harder than normal dry food and does help clean the teeth.

Many people laugh when I recommend daily brushing, but you can save your pet from having tooth pain and save yourself from costly dental procedures for your pet. It may also save their teeth and their lives! Daily brushing helps remove bacteria that can get under the gumline and into the bloodstream. These bacteria can attach to the valves of the heart, tubules of the kidneys and even bile ducts of the liver. Besides preventing tooth decay, gum infections, cavities and bad breath, daily brushing of your pet's teeth can help prevent heart, kidney and liver diseases.

Cats are prone to cavities and both species are prone to periodontal disease, gingivitis and halitosis. It is also nice to be able to kiss your pet and not be knocked over by his or her bad breath. Besides, performing a proper dentistry requires general anesthesia. It is not as if you can say, "Open wide and say 'Aah'!" In order to perform proper scaling, curetting, exploring and polishing, some form of sedation must be used.

Cats get subgingival caries, cavities that go below the gumline. To fill a cat's cavity you have to perform a gingivectomy: cut the gum, flap it back, drill, condition, fill the cavity, cure it, and then suture the flap back to the gum. Brushing teeth is much easier, safer and cheaper!

The more physical contact you have with your pet, including looking in the mouth, the more likely you are to notice any changes. I cannot emphasize this enough; the earlier a problem is detected, the better the chance for a complete cure. By brushing your pet's teeth daily, you can see possible problems in the mouth long before your pet's yearly or bi-yearly trip to the veterinary office.

Let us get back to Jillian, the puppy in exam room number one, who has been very patient while I went through my spiel with her owner. "Dr. Cohen," Mrs. Cantor announces, "I must tell you something very embarrassing that Jillian does." "Yes," I reply. "She ... she ... she eats her poop! And, it gets stuck in her teeth!" I was so glad that I had already given her the brushing teeth lecture.

Eating poop or coprophagy, as it is technically called, is a very normal behavior that many mammals do. For example, all rabbits instinctively eat their night feces to complete the digestion of their food. The bacteria that breakdown vegetable matter into digestible nutrients like B vitamins are located in the large intestine. The small intestine is where most of the absorption takes place. However, the small intestine comes before the large intestine. In order to complete the digestive process, the rabbit must ingest his or her nutrient-rich poop (night feces) to get the needed vitamins.

In the wild, many mammalian mothers will lick their offspring's anogenital region to stimulate urination and defecation. By eating the waste products, there are no urine or fecal odors to attract predators to the lair. The offspring of mammals that failed to practice copraphagy, were eaten when the moms would leave the lair to go out hunting for food. The offspring did not live on to grow and reproduce. This is an example of natural selection at work!

What Jillian is doing is instinctively normal, yet very undesirable for many reasons. Having just dewormed her, I do not want any worms that come out alive to reinfect her. Deworming a puppy or kitten, usually kills the worms. In rare situations in which there is a large number of worms, a couple could escape alive in the feces. If reingested , these worms could reattach inside the intestines and start reeking havoc (vomiting, diarrhea, malnourishment, anemia ...) all over again.

There are many remedies on the market that can put an end to copraphagy. Most of them contain a purified vegetable protein that mixed with the food, leaves a bad taste in the excrement. It obviously doesn't have a bad enough taste by itself. Adding meat tenderizer to the food can do the same thing. If all else fails, you can add Tabasco sauce to the center of the feces and cover it up with more feces. This method usually cures copraphagy, but with possible serious side effects. The Tabasco sauce can make your pet sick and cause a burning mouth sensation, so this should be saved as a last resort.

Before adding anything to the food, check to make sure that you are feeding your pet a high quality diet. Make sure there is an excellent source of protein like a muscle meat. The first ingredient on a high quality pet food label will list chicken, turkey, beef, lamb or fish. There should be no by-products, which could include lungs or intestines.

By-products are lower quality proteins. Muscle meats are better quality proteins and much easier for pets to digest. There should not be any chemical preservatives. A good quality pet food will satisfy all of your pet's vitamin and mineral requirements, as well. Sometimes, copraphagy is caused by something lacking in the diet. When pets eat things that they are not supposed to, it is called "pica." Copraphagy is a form of pica. Changing the diet to a higher quality one or adding a multivitamin and mineral supplement may be all that is necessary to resolve this.

I also instruct Mrs. Cantor to clean Jillian's ears once a week. I recommend dipping a cotton swab into a non-alcohol based ear cleaner so that there will be no burning. "I'm afraid to go in too far and rupture her eardrum." Mrs. Cantor says. Her fears are unwarranted. Unlike human ears where there is just a horizontal canal and you can rupture an eardrum if you go in too deeply, dog and cat ears have a vertical canal before the horizontal canal; they are L-shaped. "Put the Q-tip into the ear and go down as far as you can go, which puts you at the elbow of the L. The Q-tip is straight and will remain in the vertical canal, far enough away from the eardrum so as not to cause any damage." I say. Cleaning ears on a regular basis removes wax buildup, which could be itchy to your pet and lead to scratching. There are many species of bacteria, yeast and fungi that live on your pet's nails. Scratching the inside of the ear canal is an invitation for these organisms to move to this new location. The environment inside a pet's ear is a microbe's dream home: it is warm, moist and dark and any organism introduced will grow, flourish and can eventually cause an ear infection. Cleaning out excess wax can eliminate itching and may prevent an ear infection. If you clean your dog's or cat's ears on a regular basis, you will also be alerted to a problem earlier because of the change in color or odor of the discharge. Again, here is another example of how prevention and early detection can catch a small problem before it becomes a big problem.

Washing the eyes out with a cotton ball soaked in warm water or using a saline eyewash, will flush out any hair or debris from the eyes, especially in breeds with a lot of facial hair. Touching your pet's toes and getting him or her used to having the nails trimmed at an early age will also make it easier to do as an adult. An older pet will allow the owner to touch the toes, cut the nails, wash the eyes, clean the ears, brush the teeth, and open the mouth, if these things are done when the pet is a puppy or kitten. You will have a healthier and happier pet!

Now this may sound like a lot of work to do for your new pet. It is! There is not a day that goes by that I do not have at least one client telling me that he or she never did any of these things before, and the pet lived to a ripe old age. Genetics and luck do come into play. There are pets and people that inherit very healthy genes. There are people out there that live to a ripe old age despite the fact that they are smokers, drinkers, eat bacon, eggs, a buttered bagel, and drink coffee every morning, eat deep-fried, saturated foods all day long, don't eat enough vegetables, and do not exercise! This does not mean that they are doing the right things. It just means that they have inherited great genes and are extremely lucky that their lifestyle has not caught up with them.

Again, getting back to Mrs. Cantor with her new puppy, Jillian. She tells me, "Jillian has the run of the house; we are guests in her home." I don't like to hear this, especially for a puppy. "You need to puppy-proof your home. Get down on your hands and knees and look around from her perspective. She has a need to chew. If she has access to any electric cords and she bites down on them, Jillian could end up with mouth burns or in the worst-case scenario, go into shock and die."

Because puppies are teething, they have a need to chew. Because of this need, puppies must be taught that chewing on shoes, furniture or fingers is an unacceptable behavior. When your puppy is caught in the act of chewing something that is not safe, you must give him or her a firm NO! Then shove something like a large rawhide in the mouth and say in a high-pitched, positive tone, "Good girl or good boy" when his or her teeth sink down into it. It is very important to always end on a good note and teach your new pet proper, safe behavior. One firm NO is much more effective then the constant saying, no, no, no. The over use of this word has made many puppies and kittens think that NO is their name. Scolding, like any other lesson, should never be abused. Like I already said, you should always end on a positive note when placing the rawhide in your teething puppy's mouth. Rawhide is great when it is as large or larger than the puppy and hard. Once it gets soft from chewing, it must be thrown out. Soft rawhide swallowed whole can cause gastrointestinal problems like vomiting, diarrhea and can lead to an intestinal blockage.

Like toddlers, puppies should be watched all of the time. Confine your puppy to a small, safe area when you are not able to supervise. There should be a kennel or bed for him or her to curl up in, 24-hour access to fresh water, safe chew toys, a food bowl and wall-to-wall newspaper on the floor so that there are no accidents. Every week you can take away some of the newspapers to decrease the amount of floor covering until you are down to one open New York Times size thick pile. When Jillian urinates or defecates and is on the paper, you congratulate her as if she is performing the most incredible act. This lavish praise will encourage her to eliminate on the paper. Paper training is never forgotten, even for an adult who eliminates outside on a regular basis. The occasional bout of diarrhea or vomiting experienced by the older dog can be successfully restricted to the paper, if the dog has been paper-trained as a puppy.

Mrs. Cantor says, "I bought a crate for Jillian, but I thought it would be too cruel to keep her in it." This is another common misconception. A crate is a place that is just Jillian's. She can go in it to nap. You can put a blanket in it with a few favorite toys. It is the safest place to keep her when she is not supervised. "What about training Jillian? How do I go about doing it?" My favorite command is "DROP IT!" If your pet picks something up and you are across the room, by the time you get over to your pet's mouth, the item will have been swallowed already. However, if your beloved pet knows "DROP IT," all will remain safe.

One or two word commands like sit, stay, down, or drop it, work well. The first time you use these commands you must show your pet what to do and praise him or her lavishly. For example, if you want Jillian to sit, you say, "Sit," while simultaneously pushing down on her butt so that she sits. Then you say, "Good girl!" in a high-pitched tone. Food rewards work well, but are strictly Pavlovian conditioning. Ivan Pavlov rang a bell every time he fed his canine subjects. After a while, all he had to do was ring the bell to get the dogs to start to salivate. This is classical conditioning. Praise rewards operate on a higher cerebral level and won't make your pet fat!

I tell Mrs. Cantor to keep Jillian safe indoors until she has all of her vaccinations, which we will start in two weeks, when she turns eight weeks old. Vaccinations are repeated every three or four weeks until the age of at least sixteen weeks old. The reason we vaccinate puppies and kittens over and over again is because no one knows exactly when their mother's protective immunity wanes and when their own immune system kicks in. Mothers that are well-vaccinated pass on their antibodies to their offspring, thereby protecting them. When the puppy or kitten gets a vaccine and the mother's antibodies are still present, they will attack the vaccination given and neutralize it just as if it were the actual virus. The vaccine will not hurt, but it won't help either since mom's antibodies are still protective. By the age of sixteen weeks, all of the mother's antibodies are gone; so this final booster becomes very important in helping the puppy build up her or his own immune system.

Finally, I get to see the kitten waiting for me in exam room number two. Record card in hand, I greet Mr. Delaney. I first read all of the information he has filled out about the kitten. "I see here that you have an eight-week old, male domestic shorthair kitten," I say. I start examining this kitten that is here for his first vaccination. "I hate to tell you this, Mr. Delaney, but your male cat happens to be a female," I inform him. "What do you mean, Doc, he is a she? I already named him Fred and he knows his name!" "Well, maybe Fred could be short for Frederica," I say. Mr. Delaney responds, "That is not funny!" He follows with the most unusual statement I have ever heard in all my years of practice, "I thought that you could tell a cat's sex by his teeth." By the look on Mr. Delaney's face, I can tell that he was 100% serious. I very simply tell Mr. Delaney that it is much easier to just check the other end of the cat to determine the sex.

She happens to be a very healthy kitten and I see no reason why we cannot vaccinate her. I go through a very similar checklist, like I did for Mrs. Cantor, as I prepare the vaccine. I always put a baby needle on the syringe (25-gauge) right before I vaccinate pets so they don't feel it as much. I also use many distraction methods. For example, as I am vaccinating Fred on one side of her body, I have my assistant scratching the other side, while I instruct Mr.

Delaney to tap Fred's head while, simultaneously, blowing in her face. Many times, I have to tell the client to stop blowing so that he or she does not hyperventilate and pass out! Between the scratching, tapping and blowing, the patient has no idea he or she has even been injected. In fact, Fred is looking at Mr. Delaney a little strangely after all this.

I don't like needles or the pain associated with them; therefore, I do not like to inflict any pain on my patients. The various methods of distraction, when applied simultaneously, together with the use of a very small-gauged needle, give the patient a pain-free visit and a lot of attention. When the whole family comes in with their pet and I need to give injections, I will put everyone to work. While the technician is restraining the animal properly, I will have the children scratching the sides of the animal, Mom blowing in the face and tapping the head, Grandma snapping her fingers calling the dog or cat by name and Dad knocking on the examination table. Even a painful injection goes completely undetected with distractions like these!

CHAPTER FIVE

HELP!

I see my last client of the day, finish going over night treatments with the technician and head for the car. I actually enjoy the drive home because it is quiet time, the only time I have completely alone. I get to reflect on the cases of the day and relax before I open the front door.

"Hey Daddy, Mommy's home!" one of my children cheer. It is exciting to have everyone wait up for me: my husband, the two kids, and even the dog! I get to hear about everyone's day, draw a bath for the kids, and brush their teeth, even read a bedtime story to them if I am lucky. I usually pass out with one child under each arm and the dog lying across my feet. It is quite a sight! If I should awaken, I feel as if I am paralyzed; I cannot move at all. My husband carries each child to his and her respective bed, curls up alongside of me, only to have the phone ring. He hands me the receiver and says, "It's an emergency." I take the phone and before I can say, "Hello," I hear a frantic client on the other end. "Doctor, I have a serious emergency. My bird is stuck to the wall." He continues, "I just finished applying a second coat of paint in the other room. He must have gotten out of his cage while I was at the store; I was only gone an hour and now he is stuck to the wall." It is not like I can just say, "O.K., meet me at the hospital." Any kind of paint remover would probably kill the bird. I ask the client, "Is the paint oil-base or water-base?" He replies, "Oil-base." I think back to organic chemistry: like dissolves like. I suggest that he try some mineral oil, which is the safest thing I could think of. He tells me to hold on while he tries to rub the mineral oil on the wings of his stuck bird.

While I am holding, I ask my husband, "What kind of bird flies into the wall?" He replies, "Not a very bright one!" But I think to myself maybe the lights are out in that room and the bird does not see the wall. But what kind of bird would fly into a dark room? My husband's answer comes back to mind.

An elated client comes back to the phone, "Doctor, it worked; you are a genius. Thank you, thank you!" I look at my husband and say, "Twenty-two years of schooling, $150,000 later and I can unstick a bird from the wall!" Not all emergencies are that simple. There are the not real emergencies and the truly critical emergencies.

One evening, while I am in the kitchen preparing dinner, my husband hands me the phone saying, "Emergency." There is a woman crying on the other end. "What seems to be the emergency?" I ask her. "There is a tick on top of my dog's head!" she replies. I ask her, "Is it crawling or is it embedded in the skin?" Sobbing, she answers, "It is stuck in his head!" It is always best to remove the entire tick as soon as possible, hopefully before any disease is transmitted to the dog. It takes more than twenty-four hours for an attached tick to spread disease. I recommend using a fine tooth tweezer to remove the tick completely, being careful not to let the head break off. The belief that if the head remains embedded, a new body will grow back is wrong. However, if the head remains, it can lead to infection!

This woman is now screaming, "I cannot touch this disgusting thing. If I wait until the morning, will it eat its way down to the brain?" I respond as gently as possible, "There is the skull that separates the brain from the skin and I assure you there is no way this tick can burrow through to the brain." (This client really has to stop watching late night horror movies.)

There are safe products on the market that will kill ticks before the spread of disease. Ticks can spread Lyme disease, Rocky Mountain spotted fever, Ehrlichiosis and Mycoplasma. Obviously, if there is a tick on the head already, there may or may not be more on the body.

When the client comes in, I remove the existing tick and check for others. This dog has only one tick, a small localized infection where the tick was embedded and luckily no residual problems. You can get the same diseases that your dog can get from ticks. In the long run, it is safer and cheaper to use the preventatives than risk the disease.

One night, sound asleep, at 3:00 A.M., the phone rings. My very understanding husband hands me the receiver and says, "An emergency." "My puppy was retching all evening and just threw up a live worm that looks like spaghetti. What do I do?" Ms. Franklin asks.

Most puppies and kittens have parasites. They get them when they are nursing on their mom. It is always a good idea to deworm them routinely at six weeks of age and repeat the deworming every two weeks for at least two more treatments. Roundworms are the most common. Adults attach to the intestines, they can cause anemia and in worst-case scenario, death. They also present a zoonotic risk where they can spread disease to us, and can cause serious disease like blindness in children. The classic way that parasites get spread is when children play in contaminated sandboxes where stray cats have been. If a child puts his or her hands in the mouth without first washing them, the parasite eggs can get ingested and will start to hatch, grow and migrate. They always seem to end up in the eyes, but other organs could also be affected. It is an oral-fecal contamination. All zoonoses are diseases that animals can give people. Though this is rare, it does happen and is so easily, safely and cheaply prevented by routine deworming.

Fecal analyses check for eggs so a negative stool result just means there were no eggs seen and does not mean that there are no adults living inside the intestines. Maybe the adults are all male or maybe no shedding of eggs happened when the stool was taken. Whatever the reason, all puppies and kittens should still be dewormed even if there is a negative stool result.

Getting back to Ms. Franklin, who is still frantic on the phone, it is not an emergency that her puppy threw up a worm. In fact, sometimes this happens after routine deworming; the worms detach and come out in the stool or more rarely get vomited up. Where there are a large number of worms, a worm can be vomited up even in the absence of deworming. The latter scenario mandates administering dewormer. Ms. Franklin reveals to me that her puppy was indeed dewormed earlier that day in the veterinary hospital and is relieved to hear that this is a normal response. She feels better, her puppy feels better, my husband and I could feel better asleep, but educating clients is sometimes more important! The thought of a live worm squirming around on the floor could disgust anyone, but all could go back to sleep now, even the puppy!

Some emergencies are life-and-death situations. I get a phone call from someone whose dog was kept overnight in the garage. Unfortunately, antifreeze was spilled on the floor. Because of its fluorescent color and sweet taste, dogs, cats and even children are attracted to antifreeze and may lick it. Antifreeze itself is not toxic, but the liver metabolizes it into something so poisonous to the kidneys that it will put the unsuspecting victim into kidney failure. Signs of vomiting, depression, staggering, excessive thirst and urination, can happen as soon as one-half hour after a small amount is ingested. If you do not have the antidote, 4-methyl pyrazole, you can use ethanol.

For this emergency, I am fortunate in knowing that dog was poisoned because the owner went to the garage to feed the dog and saw him licking the antifreeze on the floor.

This emergency happens the first year I was practicing. I am still living at home with my parents. The hospital I am working at does not have the antidote nor is there ethanol. I put an intravenous catheter into the dog and keep the dog on IV fluids while I drive home. This is past midnight and my father wakes up to the sounds of me rummaging through his liquor cabinet. "What are you looking for?" he asks. "I don't have time to explain; just give me an unopened bottle of a your highest proof liquor." My father hands me a bottle of Absolut and I run out of the house. Driving back to the hospital I think to myself: my poor father probably thinks that I am an alcoholic or something.

I give this dog the vodka very slowly, intravenously. The mechanism of action is very interesting. The alcohol ties up the enzyme alcohol dehydrogenase, which is responsible for transforming the antifreeze, ethylene glycol, into its toxic form that destroys the kidneys. Basically, transforming the vodka instead of the antifreeze uses up the enzyme. By occupying this liver enzyme, the antifreeze can pass safely into the urine unchanged and nontoxic.

I take urine from the dog, spin it down, stain it and look under the microscope. I can see calcium oxalate crystals throughout the specimen which confirms the diagnosis of antifreeze poisoning. This is a simple test that your veterinarian can do if antifreeze poisoning is suspected.

Of course, there is no set dose to the amount of alcohol you give. Basically, I give enough until the dog acts drunk. He starts staggering, loses his balance a few times and I know then; that is enough! If you have pets and children, there is a safe antifreeze that can be purchased which is not poisonous.

A more current emergency that happened starts off with the middle-of-the-night phone call waking everybody. Evan, one of my husband's acquaintances from the television production world, calls to tell us that his eight-pound Fox Terrier swallowed a bottle of Valium. "How many pills did Scooter ingest?" I ask. Evan is unsure, but he called right after the overdose. I tell him to go to the bathroom cabinet and get a bottle of hydrogen peroxide. "Just pour it into his mouth. Make sure you get at least a teaspoon down him and wait for the vomiting to start," I advise. Evan says in such a panic that if ever he needs a Valium it is then! I tell him, "Don't worry they will be vomited up soon." And sure enough they are. Some absorption may have taken place already so I meet him at the hospital. The problem with small dogs and poisonings of any kind is that most poisons are dose:weight sensitive. A large dog that swallows a couple of Valium, a piece of chocolate, a few grapes has nothing to worry about. But a small dog like Scooter's size that eats a whole chocolate bar, a bunch of grapes or a bottle of barbituates could die. Dark chocolate is worse. Theophylline, theobromine and caffeine are the three toxic ingredients in chocolate. Grapes and raisins can cause kidney failure in dogs. Onions, avocados and broccoli in large amounts can cause poisoning. Onions can cause anemia, and avocados and broccoli can cause gastrointestinal upsets.

I put an intravenous catheter in and start Scooter on Lactated Ringer's solution. Barbiturates are rapidly absorbed so even though most of the pills were vomited up, some absorption could have taken place already. Profound respiratory and central nervous system depression can happen quite quickly. Death is caused by respiratory arrest; the poisoned patient dies because he or she stops breathing.

I pass a stomach tube and pour liquid activated charcoal into Scooter. The activated charcoal is very effective at absorbing barbiturates and many other toxins. It is a thick, black tarry substance that Scooter throws back up all over me. I tell Evan, "Don't worry, I have gotten splattered with worse!"

CHAPTER SIX

When The Time Comes

"**G**ood morning, Dr. Cohen, I think that you better take this call," says the receptionist as I enter through the front door. Coat still on, I grab the receiver. "Doctor Cohen speaking, how can I help you?" I say. "Doctor, my cat has not eaten for ten days, hasn't moved for three days, and has been cold and stiff for two days. When do you think I should bring her in for an appointment?" The receptionist has to lift my chin up to close my mouth. I am surprised that the caller's next description wasn't "There have been flies buzzing around her body!" Of course, the correct answer to his question would have been nine days ago. It was blatantly obvious that he really has no idea that she had already died. I tell him to come right in because I think it best to break the news to him in person. There are animals that die on their own and there are animals that get put to sleep.

The receptionist informs me that my first patient of the day is going to be a euthanasia. Sasha is already in the exam room waiting for me. She is an eleven year-old Husky that has been carried in by her owners because she could no longer walk. I question Mr. and Mrs. Keeros about their decision. Mrs. Keeros says, "Dr. Cohen, we don't know what else to do. Sasha cannot walk anymore and she seems so painful." I respond, "Please let me examine Sasha first before you make up your mind." I want to make sure that if I am going to euthanize an animal, it is warranted. If we cannot take an animal's pain or disease away that euthanasia becomes not only the last resort, but also the most humane option.

Sasha is very aware of me. Her eyes are focused on me as I examine her. Her head is completely normal. All of the reflexes are normal on her face, eyes, ears, nose and throat. Her heart and lungs sound well. As I move my hands along her back, she tenses up. When I get to her hips, she cries and tries to bite me. She is obviously in a lot of pain. Her x-rays reveal advanced hip dysplasia. Years ago, the most humane thing to do would have been euthanasia, but with the advances in veterinary medicine, we have the ability to turn Sasha's painful existence into one of comfort.

I offer Mr. and Mrs. Keeros the option to try some of these advances. With the exception of her hips, Sasha is in excellent shape. I took blood tests that all came back normal. Sasha is put on two different medications, one is to increase the joint fluid to cushion the hips so that the bones would not rub against each other, and the other is a very strong non-steroidal anti-inflammatory agent that will decrease the inflammation and pain.

The next time I see Sasha, six weeks later, she actually runs into the exam room and the smiles on Mr. and Mrs. Keeros' faces say it all. Outcomes like this are so rewarding, but for me, it is a bittersweet victory. I put my own dog to sleep in 1991 and hip dysplasia was one of his many ailments. If he lived today, I could have made him more comfortable and put off his demise. Spunky was a fourteen and a half year-old German Shepherd with horrible hip dysplasia, senility, liver disease, dry eye syndrome and suffered from bouts of colitis. His back legs were so bad that my mother sewed together a sling made out of my old jeans. I used to walk down the block holding his leash with one hand and the handles of sling with the other hand. It was quite a sight.

Senility or cognitive dysfunction can be treated today with medication, but unfortunately, this medication did not exist then. Spunky's senility was so bad that when I would take him out for a walk, he had no idea what he was supposed to do. Outdoors, he would just look around. Inside, he would urinate and defecate in the kitchen right after we came back from a fifteen-minute walk. He would drag himself to where his water bowl was and then fall down right in front of it. Today, there are medications that would have taken away his pain. There is even total hip replacement surgery.

When conventional medicine did not work on Spunky, I would rent a car, drive upstate and take him for weekly acupuncture. Acupuncture worked for many of my patients, but not for my own dog. I put Spunky to sleep in 1991 on my parent's kitchen floor. He probably should have been euthanized sooner, but every time I came over to perform this final act of kindness, he got better. He looked a little brighter and he never lost his appetite. My mother would plead with me, "You're not here during the daytime when he is suffering so."

It breaks my heart every time I put an animal to sleep because I know just how the owners feel. I still have the memory of euthanizing my own dog. When the day came for me to put Spunky to sleep, my brother ran out of the house screaming, "Why are you killing Spunky?" while my parents were saying, "That poor dog suffered longer than he should have!" In hindsight, I probably should have put him to sleep earlier, but he always did look better when I came over with the euthanasia solution. It was an emotional roller coaster. I can empathize with many of my clients who just don't know when the right time is.

Death is a tough subject. Euthanasia is the most emotionally difficult part of my job. At the same time, it is probably the kindest. As with every situation, there are always choices. Ultimately, the final decision is that of the pet owners. Even in the most 100% obvious situations, knowing that you are performing the most humane option is never easy.

The technician calls in my next client. Mr. Marcus brings in his beloved Ginger. She is a fifty-pound, eleven year-old tan, brown and black mixed breed dog with a hint of German Shepherd. As I examine Ginger, I see Mr. Marcus almost beaming. He is as proud of her as a new father is of his just born daughter. "Isn't she beautiful," he remarks as I examine her. I feel a lump under the right side of her chin. It is an enlarged submandibular lymph node. A few thoughts go through my head. If her teeth are badly infected, this could account for the enlarged size of the lymph node just under her jaw. This is not the case here. Ginger is a geriatric dog and neoplasia or cancer must be on the differential diagnosis list. In fact, it should be the very first ruled out. Specifically, malignant lymphoma, a type of cancer of the lymph system, can present itself as simply as one enlarged lymph node. The patient can be in perfect health with the exception of this enlarged lymph node. Diagnosis is best made by removing the entire node or just a piece of it, and sending it out for a biopsy.

A fine needle aspirate may give you the diagnosis in a much easier way without anesthesia or surgery, but the cancer could be missed because you are just sampling a few cells. The procedure is done right after the area has been surgically scrubbed. You shave the hair off and scrub the skin from the area where you are going to insert the needle. It is the same disinfecting procedure that you perform before a surgery. You take a very large needle attached to a syringe and stab the tumor deeply and then withdraw some cells. The cells are so very fragile and could be destroyed or modified during the retrieval process. Many times, I will get a report back in which the cytologist, the specialist examining the slide, recommends that I do a biopsy anyway for a more definitive diagnosis. Performing a cytology, submitting cells on a slide is more of a screening procedure, you may or may not get a diagnosis. Performing a biopsy is the ultimate confirmation, though.

I recommend that Mr. Marcus let me remove a lymph node under general anesthesia. "Could my Ginger die under anesthesia?" he asks. Anyone who says "No" would be lying. Death is always a possibility with general anesthesia, but the risks of surgery go way down if you take special precautions.

Running blood tests to make sure that there is no underlying disease, is always a good idea. Evaluating the heart and lungs with three chest x-rays and possibly an E.C.G. (electrocardiogram) are other precautions. Using cardiac and respiratory monitors, a pulseoximeter, and a blood pressure cuff machine while using a very safe gas anesthetic like isoflurane or sevofluorane, together with a high flow of oxygen, are other safety measures. Putting an intravenous catheter in the patient and keeping him or her on intravenous fluids will also decrease the risks of surgery and increase the speed of recovery. The intravenous catheter gives you an open vein if you need to administer drugs quickly like with an emergency, and the fluid infusion helps you adjust blood pressure by increasing and decreasing the flow while increasing the perfusion of blood throughout the organs.

I remove Ginger's lymph node and the biopsy comes back as malignant lymphoma, a cancer that responds well to chemotherapy. Mr. Marcus is very upset with me, the messenger. And you know what happens to the messenger. I simply report the bad news. I have to remind him, that I am not responsible for the cancer, just for its discovery. Mr. Marcus could not believe that it was possible for Ginger to have cancer. He says to me, "She looks so healthy, I cannot believe this." I hand him a copy of the biopsy report, x-rays, and blood tests and tell him to get a second, and if necessary, third opinion.

He takes the reports and the advice and sees two other veterinarians; both agreed with my findings. Mr. Marcus returns with Ginger, demanding, "I can't believe my Ginger has cancer. She is my daughter and the most important 'person' in my life. Fix her!" (Mind you, this man is married with a human daughter.)

Even though Ginger is old, she is relatively healthy with the exception of her cancer. Mr. Marcus asks all of the usual questions. "Is she going to lose her hair? Is she going to stop eating? Is she going to feel sick?" Dogs and cats that undergo chemotherapy do not lose their hair. Most of the time, they respond much more favorably than their human counterparts. The chemotherapy or chemicals change from week to week. I always administer them in the hospital. I insert an intravenous catheter, administer the chemicals slowly and allow the patient to stay in the hospital for a few hours for observation while on intravenous fluids. I take blood tests a few days later to make sure that the red and white blood cell counts are normal.

Mr. Marcus continues to ask me if my diagnosis is wrong. I ask him why he would still think this way. He responds, "My mailman and my housekeeper keep telling me that this diagnosis of cancer must be wrong because Ginger looks so good." How can you argue with logic like that?

Ginger did very well and stays in remission for two years, but when the cancer resurfaces, it comes back with a vengeance. I perform a rescue chemotherapy on Ginger that works well the first time. However, each time the cancer resurfaces, it becomes more and more difficult to put the patient back into remission. It reaches a point where Mr. Marcus, the mailman and the housekeeper all know it is time to end Ginger's suffering. Mr. Marcus cannot bring himself to end Ginger's life. He says to me, "I want to let her die naturally." After two days of watching her just lie there, not wanting to move or eat, he asks me if we could end her suffering sooner. I tell him, "Putting her to a quiet and gentle end by euthanizing her is probably the most difficult decision, but it is also the kindest."

I discuss all of the options. Group cremation occurs when many animals get cremated together, versus individual cremation where you get your pet's ashes back in a tin or urn. There is country burial where many animals get buried together versus a plot and formal burial. The owner decides and signs all of the necessary paperwork beforehand.

I actually had a client that called me up two days after I put her cat to sleep. The cat was still in the hospital freezer because she could not decide between cremation or burial. She asked, "Dr. Cohen, I know that I signed the request to euthanize Angel, but I changed my mind. Can you please defrost her and do CPR or something to bring her back?" I gently explained to her that we are not that advanced yet and could not reverse death. I assured her that her difficult decision was the kindest and most compassionate one she could make for her suffering cat.

The act itself is quick. I always administer a sedative first to make the patient more comfortable; I wait until the pet is sleeping. If the owner wants to be present, I then administer the euthanasia solution, while the dog is in the loving arms of the owner. This takes less than a minute. Mr. Marcus wants to be present the entire time. He holds onto Ginger very tightly and is pleasantly surprised that she expires so peacefully. I hand him a box of tissues and excuse myself to give him the courtesy of privacy during this very difficult moment. I struggle very hard to maintain my composure. I try to stay as professional as possible, but every once in awhile, I break down with the client.

After euthanizing a pet, I always advise my clients not to talk to people who don't have pets of their own. They often don't know the right things to say. Someone may say, "Why are you so upset? It was just a dog or it was just a cat." Some people can be so comforting while others just don't understand. I advise, "Talk to people who have had pets; they will know what to say. Sometimes, when you are talking to someone about your experience, you may notice their eyes welling up with tears as they remember their own experience."

Getting back to poor Mr. Marcus, who was having a very difficult time, I see that he keeps trying to close

Ginger's eyes, but they keep opening back up. "Why aren't her eyes staying closed?" he asks me. I answer him, "The eyes only stay closed in the movies."

Euthanasia is a privilege veterinarians have over medical doctors. I saw my grandmother die very slowly and painfully over many years. She had breast cancer, had undergone a mastectomy and chemotherapy. Then seven years later, when everyone thought it was over, the cancer resurfaced. It spread to other organs. By this time, she had undergone numerous surgeries, and suffered so recovering from each one. Nausea, violent vomiting, rawness and burning from the incisions internal and external, were just a few reactions and feelings. She became so ill from the chemotherapy, I began to question her quality of life.

I watched her die slowly. In the end, she looked like a skeleton with skin. Everything hurt. The day she died was the day she was finally out of pain. And her eyes did not stay closed either.

With any kind of terminal suffering, euthanasia enables us to treat our pets with humanity and dignity. It is one of the endless reasons that I am so grateful to be practicing veterinary medicine.

CHAPTER SEVEN

In The Beginning...

When I was three years old, my dog was hit by a car. I was with my grandmother in the upstairs bathroom; the window was open. I heard a horrible loud screeching sound, looked out and saw my dog lying in the street in front of a car. At that moment, my grandmother covered my eyes. I did not really comprehend what was happening. I do not know if I had understood the concept of death at that time, and thank goodness, I did not have to. Later that evening, I was told that my dog Bawbee (Bobby was his real name, but I could not pronounce it properly) was in the hospital and would be coming home tomorrow with a cast on his leg. The image conjured up in my mind was that of a typical cartoon. I pictured Bobby lying in a hospital bed with his casted broken leg elevated above him as if in traction. Bobby, indeed, did come home with a regular plaster cast and had an uneventful recovery. I asked many questions like, "Who put the cast on Bobby's leg and how did the doctor know that it was broken...?" This was my earliest memory of wanting to become a veterinarian. The reasons have since broadened and deepened. The desire has never left me. In fact, it has become stronger over the years.

Bobby was not just my dog; he was my best friend. He was a very territorial Cocker Spaniel. He guarded my baby carriage when I was in it. If anyone would come near Bobby when he was eating, he would growl at them; yet I hear stories about me crawling up to his bowl and sharing his dog food. We shared many a meal together. I can remember slipping him some of my dinner under the table. At such an early age, I learned about the unconditional love a pet can give you, and Bobby was my true inspiration for wanting to help animals.

My affinity towards animals grew. I remember most of my childhood getting into trouble because of my need to save the animals. Every now and then, a stray dog would follow me home from school. I fed him or her something from the refrigerator. Whatever I thought was healthy and tasty would be given; the stray would eat the meal with gusto, proceed to vomit on the living room carpet and I would get punished. This became a routine.

I had a human best friend in the fifth grade. Her name was Kerri. We would go shopping for the poor neighborhood stray cat. It was a lot of fun. We would pool our allowance money together, buy all kinds of cat food and feed the stray cat. Apparently this cat told friends, who told friends and within one month's time, it seemed as if the entire cat population showed up on my block at 3:15 P.M. Monday-Friday. Many of the neighbors complained to our parents about this fiasco. We were both punished and not allowed to talk to each other for six months.

As I got older the consequences of my actions worsened. Every year, for spring vacation, my parents took my brother and me to Aruba. There were many stray dogs on the island and, of course, they found me. The hotel where we were staying used to have a once-a-week special evening called steak night. All of the guests would dine outdoors and eat all of the steaks they wanted to. The guests would stand in line, tell the chef how they liked their steaks cooked and would wait while the steaks sizzled on the open grill in front of them. There was no limit. When you would finish eating your steak, if you were still hungry, you could stand in line again and order another. I employed my brother as an accomplice and we single-handedly fed all of the stray dogs we could. Since that vacation, the hotel has never offered steak night again.

My parents were inundated with complaints about the stray animals following me. There was a small Chihuahua mixed breed dog with five puppies. They would follow me all around the beach. It was quite a scene. The last straw occurred when they followed me, single file, of course, into the hotel lobby, into the elevator and into our hotel room. At family get-togethers, I often get reminded of how we were not so politely told to find another hotel on the island for our next visit.

In ninth grade, my science teacher allowed us to contract our grade. The more projects successfully completed by a student, the higher the grade he or she would get. If you wanted an A, you had to successfully complete ten projects. One of the ten projects involved building an incubator from scratch and hatching a chicken egg. I worked day and night on this project. I remember going to Coney Island with my father and buying four fertilized eggs. I turned those eggs over daily, checked the thermometer and refilled the water dish to make sure the humidity was just right. The incubator had to simulate what a hen would do so keeping the temperature constant at 100 degrees Fahrenheit was very important as was turning the eggs over once every day for the twenty-one day incubation period. I remember talking to a friend of mine on the phone at day twenty and hearing peeping coming from the eggs. I thought I was hearing things, but I put the phone receiver handset near the eggs and she heard it too. I knew the time was coming close. At any time soon, they were going to hatch. I had my Polaroid camera next to the incubator in my parent's living room and I slept that night next to it. At 4:00 A.M., I woke up to the sounds of cracking. You could see the beak tooth peeking up through the crack it made in the shell. Camera in hand, I started clicking away. In hardly any time at all, there was my first rooster. Because he hatched so quickly, he came out soaking wet. I named him Primmer. The second chick took so long to hatch. He tapped the shell then took a break, then tapped again, then rested. While Primmer took less than five minutes to hatch, this second chick took two and a half hours. When he finally emerged he was all fluffy and that's what I named him. This was one of the most exciting times of my life. The other two eggs never hatched, but I did not give up on them. I continued to turn them daily. After a week had past, they started to smell really bad. We gave them a funeral.

In the meantime, Primmer and Fluffy kept me very busy. We lived in a small apartment in Forest Hills and as the chicks grew into chickens, their cage had to grow as well. (Incidentally, they lived in our living room.) They were trained to come to me when I called them by name, one onto each shoulder. The one thing I was not able to do was toilet train them. I did not know that you cannot train birds that way and bird diapers weren't invented yet. I used to get punished a lot because the new carpet stains gave my parents evidence against me that I let them out of their cage again. My argument about how they needed their exercise just did not fly. Eventually they grew into large, loud roosters and it became obvious to everyone that we had to move them.

I spent a lot of time growing up in my grandparents' house and they agreed to let me keep the roosters in their backyard. My grandfather built a chicken coop for them. It was great fun. They came every time when I called them, except for when it was bedtime. I had to chase after them to put them into their coop to roost for the night. I used to get very upset when my grandfather would barbecue chicken on the grill in front of them. Psychologically, I knew that it would not upset them, but it bothered me. One day, my grandfather got annoyed seeing them on my shoulders. It was almost dinner time and he said, "Enough already with them on you!" He went to shoo them off and they bit him. These roosters were like siblings. Fluffy used to chase Primmer all around the yard for one blade of grass and vice versa. Meanwhile, there were thousands of other blades of grass right in front of them.

Some neighbors started complaining when my roosters started to eat their flowers or dig for worms in their gardens. One threatened to call the Board of Health. This was when my parents felt it was time to find a new home for the roosters. A friend of my father's came over to see them for himself. When I learned that this man had plans of possibly killing them and eating them, I ran away with Primmer and Fluffy, one on each shoulder. I hid in the backyard of one of my grandparents' neighbors until this man left. These particular neighbors were not just neighbors, but friends of my grandparents. Not only did they not complain about my chickens, they actually liked them.

Winter was coming and it was time to find a new, safe home for them. There was a zoo nearby that would take care of them. We made a small donation in their names. I was nervous about how they would like their new home, and if the other chickens in the coop would even accept them. After all, the term "pecking order" comes from the hierarchy of how chickens live together. However, if they were accepted into the flock, I would agree to let them go. I wanted the best for them.

The first encounter was interesting. The head honcho chicken blocked the entrance and would not let them pass. This head rooster was twice the size of my two roosters. But my guys were fighters, and when their entrance was blocked, Primmer and Fluffy proceeded to peck at this dominant rooster until he backed down. I knew then that they would get along with the others and would probably be O.K.. The following week, I went back to the zoo to see how they were doing. My family kept telling me that they would not remember me. Much to my family's amazement, when Primmer and Fluffy saw me, they each flew onto my shoulders, and basically roosted with me. I felt like a proud mother and knew from that moment on, they would be fine.

The following summer, I went back to visit them but I looked at them from afar, just to make sure that they were happy. That was a memorable experience.

Throughout high school, my summer vacations were always spent working with animals. While my brother was off on teen tours, I volunteered at veterinary hospitals, dairy farms and the racetrack. It was at the track, where a thoroughbred breeding farm owner discovered me and offered me a real job.

This was my first paying job. It paid ninety-five dollars a week, six days a week, eleven hours a day; and I would have done it for free. I worked with the mares and foals. The girl I replaced was killed by one of the stallions in a freak accident. This detail was left out when I begged my parents to let me spend the rest of the summer vacation working on an upstate-breeding farm. My parents would plead, "Why don't you go to Europe like your brother? He is having so much fun." I don't think my parents ever understood why I worked so hard, but they did allow me to do it.

I was having the time of my life living on the farm. It was hard work, but I enjoyed it. My duties included mucking out stalls, grooming and feeding horses, walking them out, and getting to ride them when all of the hard work was finished. The highlight of the week occurred when the veterinarian came to call. This was so exciting for me. I always stopped what I was doing in order to give him a helping hand.

Even though I got straight A's, I remember having a meeting in high school with my guidance counselor on one side and my mother on the other. My guidance counselor asked me, "So what is it you want to do with your life?" I remember seeing her face drop when I told her that I wanted to become a veterinarian. She basically told me to pick another career. Her exact words were, "Even people with straight A's out of an Ivy League school have been turned down. There are fewer veterinary schools than there are states. This makes it very difficult to get in. In fact, there are more medical schools in New York State than there are veterinary schools in the entire country. Why don't you try to do something easier like becoming a medical doctor?" Thank goodness I did not listen to her. I gained strength and determination with every discouraging word I heard.

In my senior year of high school, I volunteered at Mount Sinai School of Medicine. I made all kinds of discoveries mentoring under a wonderful research doctor, Dr. Melanie Cobb. She was the first person that actually encouraged me to follow my dream. I worked with toads' urinary bladders. The toad actually makes an ideal research model because its urinary bladder is double-lobed. In other words, it is like each toad has two urinary bladders. You can use one as a control while experimenting with drugs on the other one. This was a very exciting job for me. There I was, fifteen years old and working with medical doctors and PhD's. I tried to stay on my best behavior. However, there was this one toad that I would find hopping down the hallway every morning when I came out of the elevator. No matter what, he would escape. I had a meeting with my superiors and basically begged them to let me set him free. Central Park was right across the street. What better environment to let this toad grow up in.

I really did not give deep thought to the ecosystem, but there were other toads in the park. With Dr. Cobb's blessing and sworn to secrecy, I set this toad free. All of the research that I did that summer, the papers that were published with my name on them, the newspaper articles, even the science contest awards I had won, did not measure up to the elation I felt when I set that toad free!

CHAPTER EIGHT

School Days

Every once in a while a client will ask me where I went to undergraduate college and veterinary school. I am very proud of my education and feel extremely fortunate to have a strong background in both the liberal arts and sciences. I have a Bachelor of Arts degree from Barnard College, Columbia University. In those days, women applied to Barnard and men applied to Columbia. I majored in biology so that I could fulfill my major requirements and pre-veterinary requirements, simultaneously. This left me room to take art history, French, anthropology, English and French literature courses. I took courses that I thought would help make me a well-rounded individual. I took the maximum amount of courses allowed while working as a veterinary technician on weekends. I studied all of the time. In hindsight, the sacrifices I made were all worthwhile!

When I had a test in college, I knew the material backwards and forwards. I took a course called physiological psychology. It was a very interesting and exciting subject, but before my first exam, I had a nightmare that my midterm grade was a 34%. I was so afraid that this horrible dream was a premonition and would become a reality that I was in a panic, broke out into a cold sweat and had diarrhea before each exam. It did not matter that I knew all of the material. I just did not want that nightmare to come true. Incidentally, my lowest grade on all of the exams was a 96%, probably because of that nightmare.

I worked very hard. My A's did not come easy. In one class, they didn't come at all. When I took freshman English, I would draft my papers and write and rewrite them to try to achieve perfection, but that never came. Some of my classmates wrote their papers on the typewriter, the night before they were due. There were no computers back then, except for one very large one that took up an entire floor and had to have the air-conditioning on 24/7, even in the winter. These same students who wrote essays and comparative book reports at the last minute got straight A's. I planned ahead and did outlines. The highest grades I received on papers were A-s, but there were too many B+s so my final grade in English was a B+. However, hard work did pay off in other classes. When I took calculus, I remember spending every evening at the help center making sure that if I did not understand something, I could find someone who could explain it to me. When I took organic chemistry, I studied in the hallway of the professor's office because of the endless questions I had. I made molecular models out of pens and pencils to help me visualize mirror images. I wanted to know everything and know it well. This kind of attitude worked well for me in college. I had a hunger for knowledge that still holds true today.

Taking art history while living in Manhattan was

a real treat. Sometimes, when I had to analyze a painting, I would hop on a downtown bus, go to the Metropolitan Museum of Art, sit in front of the painting and write. In many ways, analyzing a painting is like making a diagnosis. It is all deductive reasoning. I did not know then just how helpful art history would be in helping me make accurate diagnoses. With art, you are looking at a painting trying to understand what the absent artist is telling you. You use the choices of brushstroke, colors, and subjects and try to tie together all of the different aspects of the painting into how the artist felt and what he/she was trying to evoke in the viewer. It is a very active process. It is very similar to analyzing a sick pet. You take all of your examination findings, laboratory tests, together with what changes the owner tells you and you try to put them all together into a diagnosis. The pet, just like the dead or absent artist, cannot tell you what is going on, so it is up to you to try and figure it out. This is the challenge and how exciting it is when all of the pieces of the puzzle come together into an answer.

I took my first year of French as a freshman. I always thought it was a beautiful language. My parents are from Belgium and spoke French fluently, yet they never taught my brother and me. Growing up, we only heard French spoken when our parents wanted to have a discussion in front of us without our understanding what they were saying. College French was a daily class with two hours of laboratory every week. I got straight A's in the course, but still felt that I was not thinking in the language. My essays were in perfectly written French, but they were translated from English.

The summer in between freshman and sophomore year was the first summer I took off from working with a veterinarian or on a farm and applied for a French-only speaking exchange program. I was accepted into this summer program abroad where I lived with a family in Nice, France while taking French courses there. I thought this was going to be easy. The family that I was staying with picked me up at the airport. Thank God, I had my French-English dictionary in hand. There was a lot of smiling and nodding. What a humbling experience! I was so cocky because I got straight A's in French class. I had a rude awakening and went to bed that first night with a splitting headache. The only English I spoke that summer was when I phoned home. In class, only French was spoken. At home, in France that was, the family only spoke French. When I needed a definition of something, it was given to me in French so when I thought back of that definition, I was thinking in French! When I had a dream about my French family, it was in French! (They didn't speak English.) I had finally accomplished what I set out to do.

The family that I stayed with was so nice. Near the end of the summer, they invited me to stay with them again for the next summer. I explained to them that I was only planning on taking off one summer from veterinary-related work. They suggested that I go on job interviews to set something up for the following summer and so I did. Much to my amazement, I was hired as a veterinary assistant for the following summer!

It was a very special summer. I was able to combine two of my interests: French and veterinary medicine. My French was good enough by then to converse fluently. Surprisingly, I had no problem with technical words. Medical terminology is from Latin origin. If I did not know the French word for something technical like the name of a disease, I would take the English word and put a French accent on it and voila, that would work, most of the time. I did study the year before in preparation. For example, the French word for rabies is "la rage." I knew that an infected uterus in English is pyometra. When an infected uterus was suspected, I wasn't sure of the French word, so I guessed. In French, it is still "pyometra," the same word pronounced with a French accent, of course. My pronunciation was constantly corrected. Even the French family's German Shepherd did not understand me if I asked him to get his ball because of my pronunciation. I had to make sure I was pronouncing la balle like "boll" and not "bawl" with my heavy New York City accent. When I came home to the United States and continued taking French courses, my professors commented that I spoke French with a southern accent. That made sense since I spent two summers in Nice.

Veterinary school was very different from undergraduate college. I would have liked to know everything, but it was just not humanly possible. Even, if I spent every waking hour studying, there was just too much material to know. The way I was used to studying was just not going to work. This shook my whole world to such a degree that I thought of quitting in the beginning. I even went down to the administration office to sign whatever papers I needed to. I felt that I had made a terrible mistake, and so did they for accepting me. The administrator was stunned. There were people in my class actually failing, but I was doing well. I remember coming out from an embryological anatomy exam crying. I think that I received a 40% on that exam, but what I did not know, was that was one of the highest grades in the class! This was a terrible feeling for me. I knew throughout undergraduate college that I was doing well (except for physiological psychology because I thought that premonition dream would come true), I felt good coming out from exams and I was extremely proud that all of my hard work was paying off.

Veterinary school was very different. The administrator explained it to me like this, "There is a hundred-foot high pile of material that is given to each student. You need to know approximately forty-feet worth. It is up to you to go through all of the material and come away with the most important knowledge." It was no longer the grade that mattered, but the knowledge learned. I wanted to know everything. Getting through that first year was very difficult. I threw myself into my studies probably more so than ever before. There are so many different species that you learn about in anatomy class that this is where you spend most of your waking hours. The species are different and so are the body parts. There are muscles, nerves, veins and arteries in a cat that don't exist in a dog. Some organs are missing in some species. For example, a horse doesn't have a gall bladder. The same artery and vein in one species may have totally different branches in another. The digestive systems are so very different. And you need to know them all!

You get so immersed into anatomy that you no longer see a dog walking down the street, but a series of muscles and bones all connected. I kept asking junior and senior veterinary students, "When do you see the dog again?" The answer that I was told was pretty uniform. They would say, "That doesn't happen until sophomore year when the formaldehyde smell leaves your hands!" It was really upsetting because I visualized my own dog in that same way, just seeing bones and muscles walking down the hall instead of my beloved pet. This was something that all of my classmates went through and that made it easier. We were all sharing the same experiences.

Senior year was all hands-on experiences; you went through rotations: small and large animal medicine, small and large animal surgery, radiology, pathology, ambulatory, dermatology, and ophthalmology. Each rotation lasted from two to four weeks. I ended up getting ambulatory in February. That February, Ithaca had between four and six feet of snow. I remember getting the emergency beep at 2:00 A.M., driving to some farm and the veterinarian-in-charge saying to me, "Go out into that field, palpate that cow and tell me what the problem is." The only part of my body that was warm was my gloved arm inside the cow!

I don't miss the snow or the cold, but I do miss palpating cows. You can feel everything. While your gloved arm is inside her rectum, you can feel the nodules on her kidneys, you can feel the abomasum (the true stomach), you can even feel the calf inside her uterus. You can feel the calf's heartbeat and pulse, and if you are lucky enough, the calf will suck on your fingers. (Mind you, it is really sucking on the placental wall, then uterine wall, then rectal wall, then gloved fingers.) This experience was worth it all! With dogs and cats I do digital palpation, which is very different, one finger inside the dog or cat, versus an entire arm and free hand to palpate the organs inside the cow.

Let's get back to the cow in the field in the middle of the winter at 3:00 A.M. now. This cow was in trouble because her calf was stuck and it was up to us to help her. I remember drudging back through the snow, the two hundred-foot distance, to tell the veterinarian that we had a dystocia, a difficult labor, and that we would need to get the chains and lots of K-Y jelly lube out of the ambulatory truck. When a calf has poor positioning, you have to push it back into the uterus, correct the problem, if that is possible and help it out. We repositioned the calf, tied both front legs with the chains, used lots and lots of lube and pulled that calf out!

Not every ambulatory call had this happy ending. Sometimes, you have such a badly malformed calf that would never survive on his or her own. So in order to save the cow, you have to pull the calf out, piece by piece. You use a Gigli wire to accomplish this gruesome task. You have to guard the wire in your hand so as not to injure the cow and literally saw off pieces of the calf that will fit through for vaginal delivery. This is one salvage procedure I did not experience firsthand, thank goodness!

Rotating through the clinics was all hands-on experience with supervision. There was an error made in scheduling when only three of my classmates and I were assigned to the large animal surgery rotation. Usually, there are eight students, not just four, since two students at a time need to be on call all night long. This means that normally, you would be on call every fourth night. Because of this scheduling error, I was on call every other night. 7:00 A.M. starts rounds; 8:00 A.M. starts clinics. You end by 6:00 P.M., go home, have dinner, try to sleep and then back to the clinic for midnight treatments and sometimes, emergency surgery. I remember talking to a client about her horse that was recovering from surgery. I leaned up against the wall as I was explaining the details of the surgery and then I fell asleep in mid-sentence. That was so embarrassing, but the four of us were exhausted; staying up all night every other night took its toll. At lunchtime, I used to sneak in a nap in the recovery stall, which was all padded down and dark for the horses to wake up in after surgery.

On the whole, I am very proud and grateful for my education and training. Even though I did well in veterinary school, it took me another four years after graduation, to finally read through all of the notes and know the material the way that I wanted to know it: backwards and forwards!

CHAPTER NINE

Practice Makes Perfect

In my last year at Cornell, I knew that I wanted to practice on small animals and I knew that I wanted to practice in New York City. What I did not know was if I wanted to specialize in either medicine or surgery. As a licensed veterinarian you can perform both diagnostics and surgery. In most cases, your family veterinarian does everything from taking blood and urine and analyzing the results, taking x-rays and reading them and other diagnostics. He or she will also perform most surgeries. A specialist can be contacted for more rare or complicated conditions. Your veterinarian can refer you to a board-certified dermatologist for an unusual skin problem or disease. If your pet is diagnosed with cancer, your family vet can administer chemotherapy or refer you to a board-certified oncologist for radiation therapy and/or radioactive seed implants. There are veterinary ophthalmologists that can remove cataracts surgically just as is done for people and perform specialty eye tests and other eye surgeries. Veterinarians are trained to treat the entire body and each body part in every single species, and can, most of the time. A specialist needs to be contacted for anything out of the ordinary.

If your dog is holding one eye closed, he or she may have a corneal ulcer. It could be a small erosion in the surface of the cornea from a scratch, or it could be a very large one from soap. This is why I always recommend putting artificial tears ointment, mineral oil or petroleum jelly into your pet's eyes right before a bath. If your pet shakes and some shampoo gets into the eyes, a large, painful corneal ulcer could result if there is no protection. A true ulcer has damaged all seven layers of the cornea. If your pet is holding one eye closed, call your family vet and make an appointment as soon as possible.

The diagnosis is made by staining the affected eye. Your vet stains the eye by putting a fluorescent, water-soluble dye into it. The stain will only adhere to the eye if an ulcer is present. The corneal stain is applied, the lights are shut off and a black light is shone into the eye. If there is a corneal ulcer, the fluorescent stain sticks to the damaged area and glows bright green under the black light.

There are many treatment choices. The owner can place eye drops into the eye several times a day. For very large and deep ulcers, a flap from the clear tissue covering the outer surface of the white part of the eye can be sutured over the defect. This is called a conjunctival flap. Even a contact lens can be placed onto the eye to protect it as it heals. I like to inject antibiotics under the conjunctiva (the transparent tissue that covers the white part of the eye) and right above the ulcer. I numb the eye with a topical anesthetic and use a very thin needle to inject the antibiotics. The end result is a constant trickling of the antibiotics from the hole left from the injection site over the damaged eye surface. It takes about five to seven days to completely drip out, and by that time the corneal ulcer is usually healed. This is a great method if the owner works long hours and cannot be home to medicate his or her pet. It also works well if your dog or cat does not let you place eye drops into the eye easily. If an ulcer does not heal properly, then a visit to a board-certified ophthalmologist is warranted.

To help me choose between medicine and surgery, I attended ACVIM (American College of Veterinary Internal Medicine) and ACVS (American College of Veterinary Surgeons) conferences. I was torn between the two, so I decided on a family practice to do both. The choice to see a specialist or not is up to the pet owner and the family vet. Specialists do one thing and do it well. I wanted to continue to do everything and this made me happy. I have no problem referring a case for an MRI, Cat Scan (Computerized Axial Tomography) or specialty surgery. Unfortunately, not everyone can afford a specialist. If your vet is competent to perform the specialty tests and/or surgeries, then the pet owner must decide what is best. It is never wrong to refer a case to a specialist. In fact, it could be the best option for the pet. Sometimes, the cost factor prevents this. There is no free veterinary care, but some not-for-profit organizations can help subsidize the costs because of private donations. Always call your local ASPCA, SPCA or Humane Society, if your pet needs special care and you cannot afford it.

Choosing my first job was easy. I picked a hospital in private practice where I could perform the highest quality medicine and surgery. The reason I chose a high-end private practice over a non-profit hospital was because I did not feel comfortable practicing a high volume, assembly line style of surgery. When I interviewed at one not-for-profit hospital I was told about how costs were saved when performing surgeries. By using injectable anesthetics instead of gas, by not using intravenous catheters and fluids, and by using the same sterile surgical pack on different animals, a lot of money could be saved. The patients were switched quickly and easily because they were sedated and kept on wooden boards. Saving time meant saving owners a lot of money, but I was not comfortable practicing that way. The truth is, as long as a sterile environment can be maintained, surgery can be performed anywhere. And, many times, it is. At Cornell, we performed surgery for the farmer's cat right on the kitchen table in the farmer's home. This was more than twenty years ago and a lot has changed since then.

I like all of the bells and whistles that a high-end hospital offers. The more safety features: safe gas anesthesia with oxygen and monitors to constantly check the heart and oxygen flow, maintaining an open vein with an IV catheter and keeping the blood pressure steady with intravenous fluids, the safer all procedures become. After all, every patient is someone's pet and every single precaution should be taken to keep that patient as safe as possible. I think that pet owners like the fact that I operate on each pet as if he or she were my own. I would never cut corners on my own pet. There is an oath that every veterinarian takes and thousands of years ago, the Greek physician Hippocrates stated it so well, "Above all do no harm." I take this advice very seriously.

I started off in a seven-doctor practice. I was low doctor on the totem pole and the only woman in the bunch. Being the only one of anything is hard, but I rose to the occasion. I had a great education and was taught well. I performed procedures and surgeries that the other older resident veterinarians did not and would not do and this empowered me both as the only woman and the new doctor on the block. The rule with emergencies was that each doctor rotated on each night of the week. Because I really enjoyed emergencies, the other doctors were more than happy to turn over their nighttime responsibilities to me. You could turn the pager off at midnight, but I kept mine on because the most challenging and unusual emergencies happened during the middle of the night.

I have finally achieved my life long dream of really being able to "save the animals." I was good, I was eager, I was young, I looked young and when I would show up for an emergency call at the hospital, I expected clients to thank me for coming out in the middle of the night to save their pet. Instead, I was always greeted with the same response, "Oh, Miss, when is the doctor going to show up?" Being young and a woman meant that many clients assumed I was the veterinary technician. This was very frustrating. Back then, even though female veterinarians were starting to increase in number, many clients still had a mental image of an older man as the doctor. The 1952

Norman Rockwell **Saturday Evening Post** cover illustration called "Waiting For The Vet" shows an older male veterinarian wearing a white coat and stethoscope, as he gets ready to call in his next patient. This image is what some clients still expected to find. The fact that I looked so young did not help either. Today, there are more female veterinarians than male. I am very proud that after more than twenty years of practice, I have earned my grey hairs and I am grateful to look older! However, I still get the occasional "Oh, Miss, when is the doctor coming in?"

CHAPTER TEN

On The Radio

In the 1990's I lived and worked in Manhattan and loved it. I lived in an apartment on 86th Street in the Upper East Side and worked in an animal hospital on 86th Street in the Upper West Side. In fact, I never had to leave the block! My gym, grocery store, movies and restaurants were up and down 86th Street. I treated the pets of many stars, news reporters and other powerful and influential people. I was told that the pet advice I was giving should be told to the public. I was even asked to write an expose book on famous people's pets. Everyone is entitled to a little privacy and even though my patients are pets and not children (human, that is), I felt a loyalty to keep my clients' identities private. I will admit that when my dog, Allie was only a few months old, I had to pull her away from Liza Minnelli who was petting her on the corner of my block on 86th Street and York Avenue. I apologized to her, but I was late for work. I had to wrap Allie up in a blanket and catch the cross-town bus, but that is another story.

Because many of my clients were on television and the radio, they always encouraged me to pursue a more public advice forum. Years later, I finally decided to contact WCBS 880 AM radio, the number one news program in the number one news market. This would truly be a great way to help millions of pet owners and their pets. I wrote a letter to the program director and provided sample tape recording of a few thirty-second pet reports. After several correspondences and meetings, they were going to give me a chance. I had no formal training in professional speaking for the radio which was blatantly obvious. I just had good advice and was able to deliver it in thirty seconds. The immediate response from WCBS 880 was, "Most people don't start here; they aspire to end up here!" After more meetings and trial recordings in the studio, I was on the radio. After six months, my "on air" time was doubled. I had a whole sixty seconds to deliver the most important advice to pet owners.

Sixty seconds means sixty seconds, not sixty-one or sixty-two seconds. Certain topics are difficult to cover in one minute; like teaching your cat to use the toilet, which is great if you live in a studio apartment and have a multicat household. The last thing you want are litter boxes all over your apartment.

It is quite simple to teach cats. You start off by finding a disposable tin foil pan that can fit comfortably across your toilet. You fill it with litter and gradually place it closer and closer to the toilet until one day you put the pan across the bowl and have the toilet seat down holding it in place. Once your cat gets used to voiding inside it, you start to cut a hole in the center. Enlarge the hole slowly over a few weeks time until your cat is comfortable balancing on the seat. Just like with everything there are downsides. You should never try to train a kitten or a much older cat, especially one that has arthritis. Another downside occurs if your cat has diarrhea or blood in the urine. Sometimes, diagnoses of these illnesses could be missed because gravity may draw any early evidence down the bowl. This pet report was a very difficult one to limit to sixty seconds. I am always afraid to edit too much important information out. In this case, I made sure to say that if your cat weighs too much, you would need to use two trays. Because, if your cat falls into the toilet, the training will be delayed. And, you need to use flushable litter so that your toilet bowl doesn't get clogged.

The radio topics were easy to come up with. I chose to talk about problems that were of major relevance to what I saw in the hospital. For whatever reason, illnesses and diseases seem to come in threes. I may see a torn knee ligament or corneal ulcer and then all of a sudden, find two more of them in a week. I had so many topics to write about because I chose to talk about what I saw most of. I kept the topics current. If the Fourth of July was coming up, I would talk about how many pets have phobias to fireworks or other loud noises like thunder, and how desensitization works to control these fears. During winter with a snow or ice storm in the forecast, I would talk about placing wax on and around the footpads of pets so that the salt would not burn their feet. I also talked about how booties protected the feet from the salt and any electrified manhole covers around New York City. Salt does not only burn the footpads of our pets; it eats through some of the protective rubber insulation surrounding electrical wires. Unfortunately, salt-damaged wires have been known to cause electrical shocks to some pets, people and even carriage horses.

Listeners partially choose today's radio topics. I respond to website questions from pet owning listeners and if the topics are good ones, I talk about them on the radio. I still talk about pet diseases, problems and solutions I encounter on a daily basis at the animal hospital. Still, the biggest challenge is to get as much information in as I can in only sixty seconds. The goal of my pet reports is to both inform and entertain listeners... and most importantly, lead to healthy and happy pets.

CHAPTER ELEVEN

Back To School

It is animal week in my son's kindergarten class and his teacher asks me if I would like to talk to the children about what I do. I am honored. I think it would be fun to have a show and tell with x-rays. Technically, they are called radiographs because the x-rays are what pass through the patient and through the film, creating the image. But, most people know what you are talking about, if you say that you will bring in a couple of x-rays; and barely anyone knows what you are saying, if you were to say, "I will bring in some radiographs." I bring in all kinds of x-rays of animals with ingested foreign bodies and have the children guess what kind of object has been swallowed. This is great fun for everyone.

I have an x-ray of a cat that swallowed a needle and thread, and you could actually see the eye of the needle on the x-ray. I have a large dog that swallowed a handful of pacifiers, all of which are obvious on the x-ray. The most unusual foreign object that I have is a rubber ducky whose profile was perfectly outlined on the x-ray of a one hundred-pound black Labrador Retriever. The kids have a great time calling that one.

I have an x-ray of a seven-pound Poodle that swallowed a penny. On the x-ray, you can actually make out the head and shoulders of President Lincoln. This dog needs a blood transfusion prior to surgery because of the large amount of zinc in pennies. Zinc poisoning causes severe anemia. The acids in the stomach have caused the penny to start eroding, releasing the zinc, which in turn has caused the destruction of the red blood cells. If the removal of the penny is not immediately possible, you should give lots of antacids so that the erosion of the penny can be prevented. The details of all of the above are obviously left out for the five-year olds.

I have a few x-rays of cats and dogs with urinary bladder stones. I ask the children what they think is inside the pet. It is a hard concept for kindergarten children to see stones on an x-ray, inside an animal, that were not swallowed, but instead actually formed by the diet. I bring in some samples of real bladder stones that I have removed from patients and pass them around the room. "They look like the rocks you see outside in the playground," one student comments.

Some of the stones are made up of triple phosphate. Cats that eat primarily a dry cat food with a lot of fish, milk or cheese and don't drink a lot of water tend to be the prime candidates that get this problem. In fact, male cats that eat dry food, high in fish, can be predisposed to forming triple phosphate crystals. These crystals can glue together like grains of sand and form a plug in the urethra that prevents them from urinating. These cats are literally blocked. Urine continues to fill up in the bladder until it gets rock hard and reaches the size of a baseball. This condition is life threatening and veterinary medical attention should be sought out as soon as possible. The kidneys get compromised because urine can flow back through the ureters, the tubes that attach the kidneys to the bladder. The poisons that normally gets filtered out of the body and put into the urine remain in the body and these cats tend to get very nauseous, many times presenting with vomiting as the chief complaint.

These patients tend come in with a painful belly, lethargic, vomiting, anorexic and the owner finds a dry litter box even though the cat will make many attempts to use it. They may sit in the litter box and continuously strain because they have the urge to urinate, but the crystals form such a strong plug that these cats cannot urinate on their own. Many owners will think that their cat is constipated, because of the frequent trips to the litter box. There are medications that can be given to relax the urethral muscles and more often than not, these cats have to be catheterized to relieve the obstruction. A typical blocked cat usually is, but doesn't have to be, a male, obese, stressed, on a dry food diet, and/or eating a lot of fish flavors. Some cats have all of the above and some block that have none of the above criteria. These latter cases obviously have not read the book on blocked cats. Some blocked cats have a mucoid plug. That is, there are no crystals seen, but a plug is found made of mucus. If there are many triple phosphate crystals found in the urine, the cat can be kept on an acidifying diet to dissolve them. Any diet very high in meat, like chicken as the first ingredient, can be chosen. By simply checking the pH of the urine with a dipstick, you can tell if the new diet is working. Water is neutral at

7; below is acid, above is alkaline. A pH under 7 is acidic and this is what you want if you have a cat with triple phosphate crystals. A low pH will help dissolve these kinds of crystals. There are cats that have the opposite problem. If a cat has calcium oxylate crystals, you want to make the urine alkaline. In order to dissolve these kinds of crystals you need a high pH, above 7. If your cat is straining in the litter box, anytime, a veterinary check up is important and a full laboratory examination of the urine is essential.

Repeat offenders, cats that have blocked over and over again due to crystal formation, despite dietary changes, sometimes, need a perineal urethrostomy performed. This involves making a male cat into an anatomical female. You remove the penis and leave the animal with a short, wide urethral opening like that of a typical female cat. They are male in every respect, except that they no longer have a penis. This surgery is done under general anesthesia and pain medication is used during the recovery period. It is not as bad as it sounds. In fact, these cats are so much happier now that they can relieve themselves.

Dogs can get these crystals as well. Male dogs with bladder stones have a unique problem. If they get blocked, and are unable to urinate because there is a stone blocking the urethral opening, they, too, can be catheterized to push the stone back into the bladder so that they can then urinate. Because male dogs have a bone in their penis called the os penis, they need a surgical opening made right before the os penis so that future stones will be able to drop out. The urethra may be able to expand everywhere to accommodate the stone except where the bone is. This prescrotal urethrostomy, as it is technically called, leaves an opening right in front of the os (bone). A cystotomy is performed to remove stones from the bladder. Sometimes, the whole procedure of removing bladder stones can be accomplished without surgery. Cystoscopy is where an endoscope is passed through the urethra and into the bladder. It is a difficult procedure to perform on any pet. However, if a small stone can be retrieved, an analysis of the type of stone can be determined. Then, a dietary change can be made, and hopefully, dissolve the remaining stones. Lithotripsy is used for people. This is the use of shock waves to shatter kidney and urethral stones. There are not a lot of these machines even available for people, and this procedure has only been tested on animals. This may be something that will be used in the future, as another alternative for removing stones in pets.

Obviously, I do not get into such technical talk with the kindergarten kids, but they do ask me how the stones get out and I tell them. I say, "The dog or cat is put under anesthesia, a special gas mixed with oxygen, so he or she goes to sleep and doesn't feel any pain. The hair from the belly is shaved and the area is scrubbed clean to remove all the germs from the skin. I wear a hat, gown, mask and gloves so that I don't get any of my germs on or in the animal. I cut the belly open, then the bladder open, take the stones out, and then sew everything closed. Then the patient gets woken up and can go home to his or her family." I love to pass out caps, masks and gloves, and watch the children pretend they, too, are surgeons.

I bring my stethoscope in so they could all hear what a dog heart sounds like. I place the stethoscope over my heart and have the children come up one at a time for a listen. I explain to them that a human heart sounds just like a dog heart. Seeing the expressions on the children's faces makes this a heart-warming experience!

CHAPTER TWELVE

At The End Of The Day

Ithink back to before I had children, before I met my husband, my dog, Allie, was the most important being in my life. I went to the breeder's home and saw her when she was only a few days old. I took her home when she was six-weeks old and an instant bond developed. She came to work with me everyday.

While she was still young and small, I wrapped her in a receiving blanket and got on the bus. Allie never uttered a peep. I did this daily to and from work. Once, on the bus, two elderly women asked me how old my baby was. I told them that she was only eight-weeks old. One of the ladies moved the blanket to see her face and gasped, " That's no baby, that's a dog!" I told her that she was still a baby, maybe not human, but still a baby. She did not find that comment amusing. Needless to say, I had to walk to work after that experience.

Allie loved to watch television. I know this sounds crazy to some people, but there are pet owners out there with the same experiences. Allie would sit up straight and stare at the T.V. set. Once there was an animal show on, in which a flock of geese flew across the screen. Allie ran into the next room as if to catch or see them; I was not sure which.

Because Allie loved to watch T.V. so much, I thought it would be pretty amazing to take her to the movies and see how she would react to the big screen. It was Christmas Day and I snuck her in my coat for a matinee. It was more fun watching her reaction than watching the movie. People all around were whispering, "Hey, look, that dog is watching the movie!"

The truth is at times people find pets are more important to them than it seems anything else. There have been published studies that show that having a pet can actually lower your blood pressure or help with depression. Besides, they do demonstrate unconditional love. No matter how hard a day you have had at work or school; no matter how many mistakes you have made or make; your beloved pet will greet you with excitement at the door when you arrive home, either wagging his or her tail and crying with happiness, or rubbing up next you and purring.

Some pets are more functional. That is, they are acquired originally to do a job: guard a home or store, help a physically challenged-person, be a mouser. Others are considered members of the family. This becomes a very individual decision.

My husband, Mike, was petless before he met me. On our second or third date, the weather was beautiful, the sun was shining and Mike wanted to meet Allie, who was just a few months old at the time. He thought it would be fun to take Allie with us for a stroll in Central Park. We sat ourselves down on a rock in front of the lake and talked. Mike learned then, "Love me, love my dog." We were a package deal, a team. In the middle of the conversation, Allie's Labrador Retriever instincts kicked in and she dove into the lake and began to swim away from us. I panicked. I told Mike that I would probably have to jump in and swim after her if she didn't turn around soon because I was afraid she would drown. After all, she was only a couple of months old. I can only imagine what Mike's thoughts were. Even then, he was able to calm me down.

Allie actually swam across the lake, turned around and came right back to us. I was foolishly worried that she would not have had enough energy because of her young age and thankfully, she proved me wrong. Mike laughed at the situation and me, until Allie shook water all over him and then it was my turn to laugh.

Much has happened since those days when I swaddled Allie in a blanket and took her to work with me. In those days, Allie was top dog. Then I got married, had a child, and later, another child. With each change, Allie's spirit, loyalty and companionship remained strong with me, and grew within my growing family. She is and has always been part of us. My son, Jake used to ride on Allie's back when he was a toddler. My daughter included Allie in her tea parties and Allie sat there patiently while Jamie tied a bonnet on her head and played. When my husband gets up in the middle of the night to go to the bathroom, he is still not used to seeing Allie put her head on his pillow and get under the covers. Mike who grew up without any pets has grown to love her.

Pets can enhance every life. Not only can they improve the quality of our lives, they can also teach us. Children that grow up caring for pets not only learn about unconditional love; they learn responsibility. After all, pets need to be cared for. You need to feed and walk them, take them to the veterinarian for vaccinations and check-ups, treat them when they are ill, administer or apply preventive medicine. They are living beings that positively affect everything both directly and indirectly. I have the great fortune and honor to practice veterinary medicine and surgery and give something wonderful back to the animals that have inspired me every step of the way. And ever since I can remember, all that I have ever wanted to do is save the animals.

Acknowledgements

I have so much to be grateful for and so many people to thank because I would not be here, I would not be doing what I love to do and there would be no book if it weren't for their help and guidance.

The first thank you must go to my parents, Annie and Jean-Claude Heilberg for letting me pursue my dream. From a young child to a working adult, they let me follow my heart and work with animals. Sadly, my father died before I was on the radio. He did not even know that I was writing a book and I know he would be so proud. I miss him so much.

The second thank you goes to my grandparents, Annemarie and Charles Heilberg. They picked up where my parents left off. My grandparent's house was my second home and they guided me through my early years up through my first year of college when I lost my grandmother. My grandfather died when I was in my first year of vet school, but he saw that I was on my way to realizing my dream.

Thank you, Mrs. Lucy Pospisil, my Forest Hills High School biology teacher.

Thank you, Dr. Melanie Cobb, my true mentor. With your medical and research guidance at Mount Sinai

School of Medicine, I became who I am.

Thank you, Professor Thaddeus at Barnard College for teaching me to write. Though I never did get that A, the effort was always there.

Thank you, Dr. Bob Nagell. Your friendship, emotional support and help during freshman and sophomore year at Cornell and OTS will never be forgotten.

Thank you Dr. Jennifer Koga. You were my best friend, lab and surgery partner, and study buddy at Cornell.

Thank you to every single teacher in the Vet School at Cornell. It is because of your amazing teaching that I practice the highest quality of medicine and surgery.

Thank you to every single veterinarian that has ever hired me. I have learned something from each of you.

Thank you, Crys Quimby, program director of WCBS news radio 880. You have given me the incredible opportunity to reach so many pet owners so that I can help keep their pets "healthy and happy."

Thank you, Susi Heilberg and Marilyn Cohen for being my sounding board.

Thank you, Dr. Linda Opyr. Your editing skills helped organize my thoughts.

Thank you, Jake and Jamie. You have been so patient and understanding, especially when work takes away our time together. Your compassion for animals makes me so incredibly proud of both of you!

And, most of all, thank you, Mike. You are my hero, my rock, my love, my best friend, my reader, my producer, my soundman, my videographer, MY EVERYTHING!

NOTES